OWL BE YOURS

A Magical Romantic Comedy (with a body count)

RJ BLAIN

OWL BE YOURS
A MAGICAL ROMANTIC COMEDY (WITH A BODY COUNT)
RJ BLAIN

After a wildfire took everything from her, Emily Hall made do surviving as a homeless human by day and as an owl at night. When one of the men responsible for infecting her with lycanthropy comes winging his way back into her life, she must choose between revenge or resuming a normal life.

Until Daniel's return, she never dreamed she might be able to have both.

Warning: this novella contains excessive humor, romance, action, adventure, and puns. No plots were injured during production but don't ask about the wood chipper. Some things are best left unspoken.

Cover Art by Daqri Bernardo of Covers by Combs

Chapter One

DANIEL HOLLOWS HAD INVADED my woods again, and this time, he dared to bring a dog with him. The ankle biter would inevitably scare my dinner away, and damn it all to Satan's hell, I couldn't afford to miss another meal because of him.

Instead of doing what normal people did, going home and making supper and spending time with family and friends, I survived hunting as an owl. Unless I got over myself, sacrificed the wreckage of my pride, and otherwise enslaved myself to a system that didn't care about me as anything other than an infection risk, nothing would change. By day, I played at being a vanilla, ordinary human, mowing the lawns of the rich and famous in the Bay area, pretending my life wasn't a hot mess.

At night, and over the weekends, I didn't give a hoot what humans did, especially humans like Daniel.

It was his fault I was a lycanthrope in the first place.

I still wasn't certain if he was the one who'd infected me or if one of his buddies held that dubious honor. It didn't matter; the fight hadn't ended well for me. Between the four of them,

I'd gotten in my hits before they'd accomplished their goals. I'd broken an arm, a leg, and bashed in a bastard's face so hard he'd needed reconstructive surgery to put his nose back together.

To be fair to Daniel, however much that disgusted me, he hadn't wanted a fight at all. Some life lessons I'd learned well: lycanthropes stuck together. I doubted Daniel had known his half-wit, brain-dead friends had wanted more from me than a knuckle sandwich with a side dish of crowbar.

I went for the crowbar first as often as possible. It hurt more.

Daniel walked his damned squeaky dog through my favorite clearing without a care in the world, his lean body relaxed while his bright, blue eyes keeping a close guard on his overgrown rat on a leash.

I liked rats when I could catch them. Would anyone actually miss the blighter? I could swoop from my branch and strike before Daniel realized his dog had become my prey. I stayed still, waiting.

Killing the dog would fill my belly. Despite its ankle-biter status, I preferred actual rodents, and when opportunity allowed, I hunted other birds.

Dogs and cats were safe from me—usually. But when I was this hungry, I'd eat anything I could catch, which wasn't much. Most lycanthropes had someone to teach them the ropes. Me, myself, and I tried, but I'd been lied to.

Pain wasn't an excellent teacher. Hunger wasn't, either.

As if invading my forest wasn't bad enough, Daniel sat down on my favorite log, pulled out a bag of beef jerky, and shared it with his runty ankle biter. Last week, he'd brought sausage, and he hadn't left even a crumb for me. I'd checked.

It'd been two years, four months, and twenty-two days

since I'd last eaten human food, and I missed it. I'd also lost everything I'd owned to a wildfire and lacked the proper insurance to replace much, rendering me homeless with a strip of land unfit for hunting.

I still owned the land; I'd paid it off in full with the initial settlement money I'd gotten from Daniel and his quartet of friends for infecting me with the lycanthropy virus. If I ever found the courage to report to the CDC, they could help me rebuild the broken pieces of my life.

I thought about it while Daniel fed his dog.

Choosing to wing it and live in the woods hadn't been my brightest move, but it beat admitting to anyone I didn't have a home. I survived. I could be proud of my survival. My job let me get away with a lot. The boss had installed a shower for staff to use and a washer and dryer that I used at every opportunity, and no one cared what I did as long as my work got done.

I was the first to arrive and the last to leave, which made my life easier.

As always, Daniel picked out every scrap of jerky and let his damned dog lick the bag clean.

I hated his dog, and I bet it would taste even better after its snack. Why weren't dogs on my allowed list of prey? Hunger ate at me, but I stayed on my branch, sulked, and hoped the pair wouldn't drive away my dinner.

I willed them to leave so I could get on with my night and have some hope of going to work with a full stomach for a change.

No such luck.

Daniel's half-witted, brain-dead friends showed up, and I considered doing several fly-bys and raking their faces. Brad's surgically reconstructed nose needed a few extra scars. I didn't care as much about Mike or Ned; they'd been followers in their lycanthropy party, although I doubted I'd forgive any of them for infecting me.

Well, maybe Daniel. I remembered. He hadn't wanted the fight in the first place. In his way, he'd even tried to protect me, taking a few hits meant for me. More than anything else, that had convinced me he truly hadn't wanted a fight in the first place.

He still had a scar near his right temple, a permanent reminder of his failed attempt to spare me from infection.

"Any luck?" Daniel asked.

"No luck," Brad replied, taking out a bag of jerky from his pack and tossing it to the dog. "We've checked every damned stretch of woods around here. Will you give it up already? Who cares what happened to that stupid bitch? It's not our problem."

Great. A quartet of trouble with a dog in tow had come to my woods, and they'd come searching for me. Ever since the fight, Brad had forgotten my name, calling me a stupid bitch for landing him in hot water with law enforcement and the CDC.

I'd been a different person in high school, one who still believed in hopes, dreams, and everything else the young and the foolish thought possible before life exacted its toll.

I'd wanted to be a nurse.

Those infected with lycanthropy couldn't become nurses or doctors. The risk of infection was too high.

I'd become a landscaper instead, doctoring lawns and old mowers since my preferred options had been closed to me.

Daniel and Brad glared at each other, and I thought they'd come to blows, but Daniel exhaled and shook his head. "It is our problem. No, it's *your* problem. Remember what I told you?" His tone turned so cold I fluffed my feathers and hunkered down on my branch. "You knowingly infected her. You picked a fight understanding you were contagious. You did so hoping to infect her. You wanted her for your pack. That you infected her pre-shift is unforgivable. That you're doing a half-assed job of fulfilling your parole terms disgusts me. You started the fight. You wanted her to be infected. It's your job to figure out which animal she became, bring her into custody, and finish making your amends. Do I need to remind you what'll happen if you violate your parole?"

Brad growled. "Not necessary."

"No one is going to miss a wolf if you fuck this up."

"I wasn't necessarily the one to infect her. She made us all bleed."

That I had, and I took delight in knowing Brad harbored a wolf beneath his skin. I hadn't known his species, and I hadn't cared to know. I'd assumed wolf; most were. Delight and relief coursed through me.

I'd sleep a little easier knowing I hadn't caught Brad's virus. I could forgive Daniel for bleeding on me if I'd caught his.

He'd bled for all the right reasons.

The others could rot in hell for all I cared.

Brad clacked his teeth together. "I still don't see how you dodged the law, asshole. You were there. You bled, too."

Mike and Ned wisely backed away from the two men, giving them plenty of space should the lycanthropes decide to get physical. Even Daniel's dog wanted nothing to do with the brewing fight, retreating with a whine.

In unspoken agreement, Daniel passed Ned his dog's leash.

I liked that. Maybe the ankle-biter looked fit for dessert, but Daniel even cared enough about a dog to make certain it didn't get involved. I found it somehow comforting he hadn't changed much since high school.

He'd always done things like that, aware of those around him and doing the best he could.

"Angel-verified truth. The same reason you rotted in prison once we found out what you'd done. *I* meant her no harm. *I* never intended to infect her or anyone. *I* took every reasonable precaution to avoid infection. You meant to use the virus against her as a weapon. That's why. *You* wanted to infect her, and you used us to make certain she was exposed. You knew I'd defend her. You knew she'd fight back. You knew. Then, instead of trying to fix the mess you made, a prettier girl caught your eye, so you went and infected her, too."

Damn. I'd known Brad classified as top-grade asshole, but I hadn't thought he'd been *that* awful. I pitied the other girl and hoped she'd had a better go of life following Brad.

Brad clenched his hands into fists. "It would've worked if not for you."

How disgustingly typical. Why did so many men refuse to accept responsibility for their actions? Why did they think they were entitled to the first girl to catch their attention? I'd seen through him even in high school, which had helped motivate me come time to take a crowbar to his face.

User. Abuser. Filth.

A few scars extra to go with his broken nose seemed fair. I could swoop in on silent wings and strike before any of them realized I was there. The asshole deserved it.

Daniel blew air, a huffy little snort that startled me. The sound reminded me of the disgruntled half-hoots I made when dinner escaped me yet again.

"No, Brad. It wouldn't have worked out for you. I would've

fought you for her, and I would've won. I'll still win. Don't think this is a chance to get your revenge, either. It's not."

If I judged by Daniel's tone and aggression, I was the grand prize of a cage match between rivals, and I wasn't sure what I thought of that. I'd rather have been in the fray armed with a crowbar again.

Given a chance and a weapon, Brad would need a lot more than reconstructive surgery to put him back together.

Dark fur sprouted from Brad's skin. Disgust over his lack of control, that he dared to shift into his beast over Daniel's challenge, spurred my fury. I'd been infected because of a spineless asshole.

While I had no idea what Brad's parole terms were, I didn't care. Maybe Daniel could accept them, but I never would.

Brad took a step towards Daniel, his body contorting as he became his wolf.

I took flight on silent wings, and diving down, I raked the transforming lycanthrope's elongating muzzle.

He screamed, and I loved the sound. Hooting a mocking call, I took to the sky to hunt dinner while my worst enemy's blood dripped from my talons.

THE STENCH of Brad's blood scared away the prey, and not even washing my talons helped. The asshole's virus lingered and clung to me, and the animals that should've fed me fled where I couldn't follow.

It would be another hunger-filled day at work. If I could beat down what remained of my pride and go to the CDC, confessing my status as a post-shift lycanthrope, I could get a new license and replacement bank card. I could retrieve my property deed from my safety deposit box. I could have a home.

I'd gone so long living on pride alone I froze at the thought of doing it. The CDC knew I'd been infected. Everyone knew. While I'd attended the trial in body, the shock of my confirmed infection blanked most of it out, but Daniel and his friends had all been at the hearing. They knew.

They hunted for me. Why else would they invade my forest? In time, they might even find me. The virus had changed me, even my scent, but it was only a matter of time until someone found me and discovered the truth.

I could make things so much easier on myself if I confessed my sins, paid whatever fines the CDC deemed fit for hiding my changed status as a post-shift lycanthrope, and move on with my life.

As always, I faltered at the moving on part. What did I have to move on to? I couldn't chase any of my childhood dreams. The virus barred me from doing so much. Few wanted pre-shift lycanthropes, fewer still wanted someone who was contagious, and only rare companies embraced the post-shift lycanthrope.

I lacked the prized hybrid form, which opened so many doors.

My boss believed I was recently infected, which was why I got away with working for him. He didn't care. If anything, my infection status made his life easier. The virus ensured I'd recover from a work accident quicker than vanilla humans, and as long as I neutralized any blood I shed, he viewed it as an acceptable risk.

He even kept a fresh stock of neutralizer on hand and in my truck if I needed it.

To keep the workplace peace, he kept quiet about my status as a lycanthrope.

Maybe I couldn't move on with my life, but he'd given me some peace and a life with purpose, allowing me to pretend I belonged.

I hated Mondays more than most, although I pretended I enjoyed them. No one would understand. My failed hunts over the weekend would leave me shaking with exhaustion by Friday, and I'd drink as much water as I could to hold the hunger pangs at bay.

As always, I was the first to arrive, raw from my typical shift a few blocks away. My clothes had survived being stashed for the weekend without incident, much to my relief. I took a quick shower and began my weekly ritual of guzzling enough water to trick my stomach into believing it was full. The tedious process of loading the mowers and other tools onto the trucks would eat up most of my morning and keep me busy.

Handling the entire fleet of ten vehicles earned me the good will of my fellow co-workers—and made the few who suspected I was infected look the other way.

If I could just replace my bank card, everything would be all right, but I needed a new identification card to do it. One raging wildfire had taken everything. A single stop at the CDC would fix everything, if only I were willing to talk about the day Brad had robbed me of my humanity.

I'd gone through one trial.

I refused to go through another.

I clung to my new-found consolation: Brad hadn't been the one to infect me, although I wondered if the virus I harbored had been so repulsed by the bastard it had mutated into a different species.

I'd only met wolf lycanthropes, and whenever I smelled one, I avoided them. The confirmation Brad was a wolf reinforced my choice.

The entire lycanthrope race could kiss my ass. Thanks to Brad, I'd die old—extremely old—and single.

And a virgin.

The day my infection had been confirmed, I'd made a choice: I would rather die than infect someone else.

Muttering curses, I ran through my equipment checks before returning to my truck, hopping into the cab, and starting the engine. The diesel growled, and while it warmed, I went over my list of jobs for the day. I expected regular customers on a Monday, but I didn't recognize a single address on my list.

Daniel in my woods was a special sort of hell. Brad and company was the worst sort of hell. A full roster of new clients was a living hell I wanted to escape.

"What the actual fuck is this?" I howled, sliding off the seat, standing on the bar step, and waving my clipboard in flimsy defiance.

My boss strolled onto the lot, dressed in his usual overalls, ready to conquer the properties of his wealthiest clients. He raised a bushy eyebrow. "Your client list for today, Emily. Pat's out with the flu, so you have part of his schedule. Isham's so hungover he might still be drunk, so you got his critical clients for today. I've got you on extra hours tomorrow to give you a chance to catch up on your roster. Fit in what you can. If you can run late tonight, I'll authorize the overtime."

Normal people liked overtime; it bought luxuries and made the bills easier to pay. Me? I ended up with fewer hours to hunt dinner. After I got off work, I'd hunt as normal, hope I caught something for a change, keep the damned pellet, and drop it on Isham's head. I'd buzz him a few times, too.

That would teach him.

"Is there anything I should know about these clients?"

"Your three o'clock is obsessed with inviting the hired help in. If you work fast, you might dodge her. If you don't, good luck. She'll try to feed you. Isham got food poisoning from a cupcake."

Damn it. I'd finally gotten a job with the sacred dessert offerings and it came with the risk of food poisoning? Would it be worth it?

I couldn't remember what a cupcake tasted like.

"Anyway, there's a gentleman in a suit out front who wants to talk to you. I told him you had ten before you hit the road. He wouldn't tell me what he wanted, though."

My boss believed in walking the straight and narrow, and he associated gentlemen in suits with official matters. Unless I dealt with it, he wouldn't leave me alone about it. If the man needed to see my license, I was fucked. My boss had a strict rule: a single ticket in one of his trucks, and it was an instant fire. He'd looked over my license before the wildfire and hadn't asked about it again. When he did, I'd either be forced to go to the CDC or give up playing human altogether.

I grunted, dumped my clipboard on the seat, and headed for the front lot to deal with my unwanted guest.

I wasn't sure which one of us was more surprised: me or Daniel.

Shit, shit, shit.

"Emily Hall, if my eyes don't deceive me. It's been a while."

My entire body tensed. "Not long enough, Daniel. I'm about to go on shift. What do you want?"

Ignoring my less-than-pleased tone, he closed the distance

between us and pulled out a badge identifying him as an FBI-CDC liaison. "I'll call someone in to cover your shift, but I need to ask you some questions."

Daniel had joined law enforcement? My tension grew into stomach-cramping dread. "Why?"

"I was hoping we could skip the hostility. I know you don't have any reason to welcome me with open arms. You were infected with the lycanthropy virus. We both know it. We went to court over it, and I was there at the hearing confirming your infection." He sighed and returned his badge to his pocket. "We don't have any current data on your virus levels, and we were unable to find recent residency information. I was assigned to your case due to our history."

I took my time looking him over. In high school, he'd made no secret he'd been infected with the lycanthropy virus at birth, and everyone who'd been in classes with him knew his parents had the hybrid form; the public register made an indication of status including the probability of developing the prized hybrid form. Daniel had been listed at high odds due to both of his parents having it.

He'd turned heads wearing jeans, but he cut a clean figure in a suit, which likely made him a top bachelor in the lycanthropy community—or already mated.

I refused to fall for the trap of his pretty face and relaxed stance. "As what? Arch enemies?"

"Friends."

I hesitated to call our high school bickering friendship, but he had stepped in the way of a few hits meant for me. I also remembered what he'd told Brad while scaring off my pray. "It's a bit of a stretch, but I'll let you get away with it this once. I really do need to get to work. I have the crazy cupcake lady today."

If he came between me and the chance of food poisoning from eating something meant for human consumption, I might pick a fight.

Daniel chuckled. "I'll have a replacement brought in for you. The CDC keeps a staff of employees on call in all major metropolitan areas for cases like this. It'll take a contractor less than half an hour to arrive, and if you have a long shift, a second one will come in to make certain all your work is covered."

Shit. I'd heard his confident tone before. Whenever it cropped up, he knew he would be getting his way no matter what. "You're really not going to take no for an answer, are you?"

"I'm afraid not. I've been looking for you for a long time, Emily."

Had he been hit in the head a few too many times as consequence of working with the FBI and CDC? I considered my options. Bailing seemed wisest; I could open the bathroom window and be winging it out of town as fast as I could fly before he figured out I'd given him the slip.

No one knew I could shift.

"I need to use the bathroom and tell the boss."

"In high school, you had a bladder of steel and only used the bathroom whenever you wanted to escape out the window. CDC's headquarters is a ten-minute drive from here. I'll go with you to tell your boss and give him the number to request a contractor or two depending on your workload."

Damn it. He remembered that? I'd used the window a few times on him after heated arguments. "I'm far too old to be climbing out of any windows."

I'd fly out like a dignified being.

"I'm not buying that. You're tricky. I'm not letting you out of my sight *or* near a bathroom with windows."

"A person can't climb out the bathroom windows here."

"See? You checked."

Shit. I had. Many times. I'd even rigged the one window to open with some beak and talon action in a pinch. "I'll show you the bathroom myself if need be."

"You'll survive until we're at headquarters. I'm not going to underestimate you. If you escape now, it might be another ten years until I get lucky and find you again."

I struggled to believe it'd already been ten years. Brad had masterminded his attack to happen at our high school, forcing me into the system in the first place. Brad, Mike, Ned, and Daniel had been registered as the instigators, although Daniel had walked clean because he'd been the only one willing to testify in front of an angel.

I'd been there for that hearing, but like the rest of my memories of the trial, they slipped into the shocked haze.

I'd lost so much but gained nothing for Brad's machinations. My graduation had been soured by the confirmation of infection, every last one of my dreams crushed by the one thing I couldn't conquer with good grades and determination.

I'd lost my acceptance into college and gained a registration in the CDC's databases instead. I'd been projected to have a thirty-year incubation period, but living on my own, outcast because of hatred and fear, had jumpstarted my virus.

Instead of dying in the wildfire, one that'd developed without warning, I'd flown over the flames on silent wings.

I surrendered to the inevitable with a sigh. "Fine."

I could escape out the window at the CDC as easily as I could out the bathroom. With Daniel hot on my heels, I went to inform my boss I had an unwanted date with the CDC.

Chapter Two

DANIEL GOT me into his SUV, locked the doors, and targeted me with his best smile. The unpleasant part of the lycanthropy virus kicked in at full force along with a serious case of lust.

The need would pass in a few hours. It always did. Until then, I'd do my best but would ultimately look Daniel over like he was the main course at dinner. My virus had a mind of its own, and when men smiled at me, it got ideas. When pretty men like Daniel smiled at me, it got ideas it wanted me to pursue immediately if not sooner.

It had been a while since I'd endured any reminders I wasn't quite human anymore and lacked a mate. As I did every other time my virus wanted me to pick a male, settle down, and enjoy having a few important needs fulfilled, I turned my head so I wouldn't have to look at him, taking calming breaths until I could relax.

Daniel chuckled. "I can smell your interest, Emily. Your virus is maturing. That's good. Don't be embarrassed. It's natural. Your virus is just telling you there's an eligible partner nearby."

"My virus needs to be reeducated on the definition of eligible."

He started the engine, but he didn't drive me towards my personal hell, the one where I'd have to confess I'd been shifting for years and had broken more laws than I cared to think about. They might take pity on me and give me a new card, make sure my license was up to date, and otherwise help me take back my life, but my pride already hid waiting for the worst.

"I tried to stop him, Emily. I'm sorry. If I'd known his intentions, I would've kicked his ass and handed him over to the CDC myself. It's why I became an agent. My job is to help people like you. You haven't renewed your driver's license. You haven't made a single withdraw from your bank account in over two years. We weren't sure where you worked, as your employer has multiple businesses all over the country. Your company's based in another city, and your mailing address led us to an empty lot. I thought you'd gone full animal. It happens sometimes. I'm relieved I was wrong. I was running out of Emily Hall leads to check. There's fifty of you in the state."

I refused to cringe, and I refused to lower my chin and let the shame of having wandered aimlessly for years best me. "Your friend was just a bully wanting a fight," I replied, aware of the truth but unable to admit it without giving away I'd seen his dispute with Brad.

"He was a bully who wanted to infect you with lycan-thropy so he could claim you as his mate. You were at the hearing, same as me."

One day, maybe I'd find the courage to admit I'd blocked

out most of the details. I remembered Daniel being there. Something about his expression had bothered me. The rest blew away like the faint haze of smoke on the wind.

I knew all about smoke on the wind.

"He's an asshole," I grumbled. I'd save all my pellets and stalk the bastard, bombing him with regurgitated fur and bone. "If he comes near me, I may very well try to kill him. Please provide a crowbar. I don't have one anymore."

"FBI agent," Daniel reminded me.

"Quarter of the reason I'm infected," I countered. While I was an owl, I managed a decent growl. "I would've rather been left alone, you know. I had the crazy cupcake lady today."

"With no valid identification and no home address? Give me a break. You're smart to have gotten away with it for as long as you have. We can get you legalized again. Hell, with that disappearing act you pulled, you might even get a fast-track to being hired. The FBI and CDC is always looking for smart people who can vanish without a trace."

I frowned, took the risk of encouraging my virus, and glanced at him out of the corner of my eye. "I lost everything in a wildfire, and I refuse to be poked and prodded like some freak because a pack of lycanthropes picked a fight and infected me."

I wondered if the truth would set me free, and I waited for the verdict.

"There's one poke, and it's to check your virus levels. That's it. You'll be asked a few questions, including specifics on any relationships you've had since infection."

I bristled at the implication I might've infected someone else. "There's no one. No relationships, no friends. I'm a loner. Happy?"

"No, I'm not happy. Lycanthropy doesn't mean you have to

live as a hermit or outcast. If I'd known you'd been infected before the hearing, things would've been different."

"I still would've been infected. Not a help, Daniel. Lycanthropy is an incurable disease."

"You wouldn't have been alone."

I snorted. "Better alone than with an asshole like Brad."

"You would've been with me."

There were several ways I could interpret his reply, and all of them unsettled me. I remembered his argument with Brad and his claim he'd fight for me.

I just didn't understand why.

ON THE OUTSIDE, the CDC's office looked like every other corporate building in Walnut Creek. It took a lot longer than the ten minutes promised, and as though convinced I'd give him the slip, he parked in the underground garage to cut off my easy routes of escape.

I wondered why the building had an underground garage when there were outdoor lots available. Judging from the way Daniel drove, he had an assigned spot.

I fidgeted, and Daniel tried to charm my virus with his smile. "You can relax, Emily. You have nothing to worry about. The last thing the CDC wants is a startled, anxious lycanthrope rampaging. Your driver's license can be reinstated along with your bank card, and I can help you find somewhere to stay in the meantime if it's an issue. The cards won't take long, though—you should have them by the end of the day or tomorrow morning at the latest."

"I'm not helpless. I've been getting on just fine, thank you."

My traitorous stomach chose that moment to gurgle and

remind me I hadn't fed it anything other than water in days. The water I'd guzzled in the morning came perilously close to escaping, and I swallowed several times to keep it where it belong.

Throwing up wasn't on my list of things to do, and neither was collapsing in an exhausted, shaking heap at Daniel's feet. Unless I got my act together, someone would be scraping me off the pavement.

"You're tired, stressed, and judging by how upset you became over the loss of a cupcake, you're hungry. Cut yourself a little slack. The hunger problem's easy. As soon as we're upstairs, I'll send someone out to get you something. You're also welcome to share my hotel room with me, too. There are two beds, and you'll enjoy the tub."

If my virus had its way, one bed would have an unfortunate accident, then his clothes would have an accident, too.

He needed to stop smiling at me and giving my virus ideas. I choked back a whimper founded entirely on my unreasonable desire to let my virus have its way for a change.

"What's your favorite food?"

His question doused my unreasonable interest in him as effective as a bucket of ice water dumped over my head. Shame over my diet cut off my breath, so I shrugged.

"All right. Maybe we should address this before we go upstairs. Why do you smell like you've been caught stealing candy from a baby?"

I clenched my teeth and wished I could disappear.

"It'll be easier if you tell me. If you don't want to talk about it, I can speak on your behalf."

Pride came before the fall, and I had a lot of falling to do, and I couldn't see any way out of it. Steeling my nerves, I choked out, "No one likes admitting they're homeless."

"Already knew, Emily. You virus has matured enough for you to shift, hasn't it? You don't have access to your money, hunting's free, and you don't have a home. When was the last time you've had a good meal? As a human, I mean."

"It's been a while."

"How long?"

I scowled, considered telling him to leave me alone, but decided to test his claim he meant to help. "Two years."

His smile made another appearance. "What species are you?"

Fury over what Brad had attempted goaded me into snarling, "Not a fucking wolf."

His smile brightened. "You didn't inherit Brad's virus? Good."

On that, we agreed. "I really will kill that asshole if given a chance."

His chuckle intrigued my virus even more than his smile did. "You don't want his virus anyway. He'll never have the hybrid form. I do. I know what you are, Emily. I've seen you. I've no intention of letting you get away, either. Not this time."

PANIC SHIFTING LED to all sorts of problems, including becoming tangled in my clothing and falling out of the SUV. I smacked into the pavement hard. I flopped around with the same general grace of a drunk at the tail end of a three-day bender. It hurt. Worse, it cost me time.

Without a care in the world, Daniel got out of the vehicle and dropped his jacket over my head. "All right. I underestimated your flight instinct a little. Take a moment and get control of your nerves. I'd rather not give you a heart attack."

I scoffed at the idea of having a heart attack after being alarmed into shifting. Covered with his jacket and tangled in my clothes, I made an easy target. Daniel began by pinning my wings to my body. I clacked my beak in frustration.

"This would've been a lot easier if you'd just walked upstairs instead of being stubborn."

Did he expect anything else from me? I'd been stubborn from the day I'd been born. I hooted at the insult I'd roll over just to make things easier on him.

"Don't get mouthy with me. You're the one who thought shifting in the car was a good idea. You hit the ground hard, too. If I let you fly off now, you'll run right into the wall. How do I know this? I've lost count of the number of times I've crashed into a wall. We're not suited for indoor flights."

While I had several calls at my disposal, only my saddest hoot would do.

"I'll have someone fetch you as much raw meat as you can swallow if you promise to behave long enough for me to carry you upstairs. If you're good, I'll get you an entire box of cupcakes you can make yourself sick on in my hotel room."

I shook out my feathers in my cage of clothes and wished I had a way to inform him it'd take more than a few cupcakes to lure me anywhere with him.

"How about a nice grilled steak, too? My hotel makes them. I'm hoping I'll be assigned here for a while because of the room service."

A steak went a long way to convince me to go somewhere alone with him, even into an alley. Add in an entire box of cupcakes, and I'd do so without a fuss. I issued a more

demanding hoot to discover what other food he might bribe
me with.

"Lobster."

It was a damned good thing owls couldn't drool.

"I see that got your interest. Here's my current offer: I'll
provide you with a steak, lobster, and an entire box of
cupcakes for your enjoyment, but you need to cooperate. I'll
carry you in your clothes and my jacket, so try not to shred
everything with your talons."

When I didn't protest, Daniel gathered me in his arms and
rose to his feet with a grunt, carrying me off with no evidence
of being burdened despite my large size.

Damned lycanthropes.

ALL DANIEL HAD to do to get people to leave him alone was
inform them he was escorting a cranky lycanthrope female. I
wasn't entirely certain if mentioning my gender or species did
the trick, but it worked. After a long, uncomfortable hike,
which included a few too many sets of stairs, he put me down
onto a wooden table.

"You said you were checking out a lead. Why is your coat
wiggling?"

My virus didn't like the presence of a rival female, and I
clacked a warning followed with my most menacing hiss.

"My lead was a hit, and I startled her into shifting in the
parking garage. I didn't have a bracer or hood with me, and
she got tangled in her clothes. It was easier to carry her up
here. Honestly, I doubted I could get a hood on her even if I
tried, but you know how the uppers get. Hood the cranky

birds with beaks. I'd like to see them start muzzling the wolves."

The woman chuckled. "They've been trying to pass muzzle laws for years. It'll never work. And you know full well they've never managed to get a hood on you, either. She's an Ural owl?"

"As a matter of fact, yes."

"You don't have to look so damned smug about it."

I didn't know what expression Daniel made, but smug over me being an owl worked in my favor and put me above the rival female. My virus approved of an elevated ranking. I had no idea what an Ural owl was, but I assumed they were talking about me.

"Yes, I do," Daniel replied. "She accepted an offering of steak, lobster, and cupcakes to come with me to my hotel room tonight. I'm hoping I'll be able to extend the invitation tomorrow until I'm able to find her a nest she can settle in properly."

"You got off light."

"I'm pretty sure it's only the beginning. I might have to offer Brad's head on a platter to get her to trust me."

"I'm game. Do you need the rest of his body to appease her wrath?"

"Good question."

"So, this is your high school sweetheart that that ass infected during a fight? How'd she contract *your* virus?"

"High school sweetheart is a stretch, and I took a few hits trying to protect her."

Well, I gave credit where credit was due; Daniel didn't shy away from the reality, and I appreciated the closure of knowing for certain he'd been the one to infect me—and it explained my virus's keen interest in him, besides a bed and a lack of clothes. I'd heard the lecture.

Like called to like, and my virus would want someone of the same or similar strain. It wouldn't surprise me if his virus acted the same way, drawn to mine like a magnet.

The woman hummed. "You bled that much?"

"Yeah, I did."

"All right. Introduce us."

Daniel began the tedious process of extracting me from his jacket without ruining it. Once he freed me, he shook his head at the mess of my clothes. "Miranda, this is Emily."

Miranda wore a blazer and silk blouse, the kind I expected from a wealthy business woman ready to conquer the world, so far out of my league I wondered why she bothered staying in the same room with me. If she got a good look at my grease-stained fingers, dirt likely lodged under my nails from my morning prep work, and gaunt frame, she'd laugh me right out of California.

"Pleased to meet you, Emily. Don't let Daniel be too much of a pest. You're encouraged to put him in his place if he bothers you."

Daniel grunted, and he raised a brow. "Emily, Miranda is another woman Brad infected. She's a lawyer, and she's made it her life's mission to make Brad as miserable as possible."

I tossed my initial impression of the woman right out of the window and upgraded her to a potential partner-in-crime. A lawyer could advise me on how best to kill someone —specifically, Brad—and get away with it.

"You may as well tell her the rest," Miranda stated.

"When she's not making him miserable, she pretends he isn't her mate. One of these days, she's going to kill him, and I'll be the poor bastard stuck with the investigation."

Miranda secured her place as my favorite person on Earth, a staunch ally in my quest to ruin the man who'd ruined both our lives. I cocked my head to the side and watched her.

"He deserves it. Take it from me, Emily. As far as lycanthropes go, Daniel's not bad at all. I might've taken him if he hadn't been so set on finding you—and Brad hadn't been a determined, cheating bastard of a wolf. Lycanthrope males are pests to begin with, and they play for keeps. I look forward to the day I bury my so-called mate so I can find a real man. Unfortunately, I haven't been able to convince Mr. FBI here I'd be doing the world a favor. I'm hoping someone else tires of Brad and kills him so I can bury him."

Until Miranda, I hadn't met someone with the same chip on her shoulder as mine, and I watched her with interest. I broke laws every day, especially on the lycanthropy virus front. I confessed my status, somewhat, when asked, but I dodged the mandatory testing and had neglected to inform anyone I'd undergone my first shift.

Thanks to Daniel, I'd never be able to hide the truth again, and I wondered how much my life would change.

"Come on, Miranda. Don't give her ideas. She already tore his face up again. She really might kill him if she gets a chance. How the hell am I supposed to investigate *her*?"

"You don't. We pitch justifiable homicide, I try the case, I use our mutual status as unwillingly infected, and she walks with a token slap on the wrist at worst. It's true he infected her."

"With my virus."

The bitterness in Daniel's voice startled me into hooting. After his speech, I'd believed he liked the outcome. My virus certainly liked him. It made sense, however.

His virus had become mine.

"I think you're approaching this the wrong way, Daniel. Emily, he's more of a gentleman than my worthless mate. Don't let him deceive you, however. He would've infected you—"

"Miranda!"

I fluffed my feathers and hopped across the table out of reach of the raging lycanthrope.

"Daniel, don't be an idiot. It's important she knows the truth. If you want her to become your mate, start with telling her you'd planned on winning her long before Brad targeted her. That she never learned about your—"

"Miranda!"

"Thank you for reminding me I have a name. Stop being a baby. Emily, the man's had a crush on you since he discovered girls were pretty instead of cootie carriers. He's been checking into every Emily Hall in the entire damned country trying to find you. He drags me along to help him with the legalities and keep Brad in line. Brad owes you a substantial amount of money due to infecting you. I realize you've received the first lump sum payment, but the rest owed has to be signed for in person. I tried to have that overturned, but I haven't had any luck so far. He's had his wages garnished since the day he was sentenced to pay out what you're owed. No pity from me, either. The CDC pays me a stipend to put up with him. Please feel free to kill the bastard at leisure so I can court a wolf worth my while. My virus is developed enough leaving is not an option."

Daniel sighed and lifted his hand to pinch the bridge of his nose. "You're chatty today, Miranda."

Miranda pointed at me. "She beat his face in with a crow-bar. As far as I'm concerned, she's my best friend for life. *I* haven't shifted yet, and I hope that fucker'll be long dead before I do."

"Unless he directly violates his parole or forces you, we can't do anything about it. And should he, I'll testify before an angel while picking his fur from my talons."

I hooted, lifted my leg, and showed off the curved daggers attached to my toes.

"You can help," he promised.

If Daniel was trying to get on my good side, he was doing an admirable job of it. Revenge might give me a chance to accept the infection I couldn't cure *and* rid Miranda of the asshole permanently. I savored the idea enough I fluffed my feathers, hopped towards Daniel, and issued several demanding hoots.

"We can discuss it after you've been fed. Miranda, according to her, it's been two years since she's eaten as a human. She's pretty gaunt. While she showed interest in my offerings, I'm worried she'll get sick. Thoughts?"

"Wait. Two *years*?"

"No license, no bank card. She's been shifting and hunting at night and over the weekends as far as I can tell. I found where she was nesting, but the boss confirmed my worries before I picked her up this morning: her hunting grounds have thin pickings at best."

"Do you want to try her on raw or live meat? I can send someone to the pet store for feeder mice. If she's been hunting, pellets aren't going to bother her."

"I want her to be human," Daniel snapped.

Miranda's brows rose. "Easy there, Mr. FBI. Maybe you need a few steaks to take the edge off. Ask her nicely to shift, give her some space, and wait to see what happens. I really don't know why you're asking *me*. I can't even shift yet. It'll be at least another ten years before I'm ready. Frankly, I'm more concerned she's shifted so far ahead of schedule."

"Do or die. She got caught in a wildfire. And anyway, she has every reason to hate me."

"If she hated you, she wouldn't be waiting patiently for you to feed her."

Miranda made a very good point, and I wasn't sure what I thought about that. My relentless hunger didn't help, as it insisted on gnawing at me. Could I get away with a light nip to inform Daniel he needed to live up to his promise to feed me?

"All right. Emily, please shift. I'll be right outside if you need anything. Just give a hoot or holler if anything's wrong." He rose to his feet and headed to the door, hesitating before reaching for the knob.

"Good grief, Daniel She's a lycanthrope. She's hungry, not on the verge of death. Relax. You can leave her alone long enough to shift and get dressed. While you're fretting, I'll go find her something to eat and call for a doctor. She's going to need more than a virus scan, and a doc will let me know what to give her."

Daniel twitched. "Maybe I should take her to my hotel room instead of doing this here."

"So you can get territorial? No, Daniel. You can entice her with bribes after she's gotten something to eat and she's been checked over. Honestly, if she's as starved as you think, she's going to be sleeping it off. You're just going to have to wait. Emily, smack him around if he enters your personal space without your permission. You have a lot of legal leeway as an unmated lycanthrope, and I know every loophole in the system should you need them. Daniel's going to hover. That's what interested unmated lycanthropes do."

The entire exchange baffled me, especially when Daniel stormed out of the room. Miranda chuckled and followed. "Don't mind him, Emily. He's a lycanthrope. Lycanthropes like him are driven to protect. It's their role. Your role is to kick his ass whenever he oversteps your boundaries. He'll hover until he thinks you're back on your feet."

"Hoot if you need me," the man in question demanded from the hallway.

Miranda left and closed the door behind her. What did Daniel think I'd need help with? I found it absurd he thought I'd need help with anything. It'd taken me a few hours to figure out how to become human again after fleeing the wildfires, but I'd gotten to the point I barely had to think about it to trigger the flash of pain and the disconcerting lurch as I shifted from an oversized owl to human. My clothes hadn't emerged unscathed, and I sighed over the new holes in the fabric.

I should've been grateful the tears were in acceptable locations. Once clothed, I considered my escape routes, of which there was exactly one: through the door where Daniel waited.

While tempted to run so I could test his willingness to chase me, I accepted the reality of my situation. Even if I ran, he'd catch me without much effort.

I smoothed my clothes the best I could, lifted my chin, and said, "I don't need help shifting, you know."

My words summoned Daniel, who closed the door behind him. "Good. Honestly, I expect you're better at shifting than most. Your virus developed a lot faster than expected, too."

"It was either shift or burn to death," I reminded him.

"I'm sorry you lost your home."

"Shit happens."

Taking a seat across from me, Daniel looked me over and

sighed. "Can you handle answering a few questions? If you need to settle in and get something to eat first, just tell me. I don't think this'll take long, but it'll keep the paper shufflers happy."

"Heaven forbid we disappoint the paper shufflers."

"Exactly. They're vicious when thwarted."

"What are your questions?"

Daniel clasped his hands in front of him on the table, and he alternated between clenching his fingers until his knuckles turned white and relaxing his grip. "Why didn't you have your cards replaced?"

Did he really not understand why I wouldn't want anyone to know I'd shifted? Then again, he had the hybrid form. He had options. "It was hard enough keeping a job while infected. I'm too much of a liability without a pack." I wrinkled my nose at the thought of being a bird among wolves, a target because of my gender and lack of a mate. "Everyone always assumes I'm a wolf."

"Ural owls are rare. You're one of twenty in North America. Unlike traditional lycanthropes, our species has a tendency to engage in long courtships. Most pairs only have one or two children, and the odds of passing on the virus is slim. This might comfort you: it's harder to catch the infection from one of us. I was infected before birth, which puts me as an oddity, too."

"I still managed to catch the virus." Somehow, I managed to keep my tone from turning bitter.

I accepted Daniel hadn't been at fault, and I believed him when he claimed he'd wanted to protect me. I suppose he had; catching his virus far surpassed being burdened with Brad's.

"Brad's the kind who wants what others have—or wants to stop others from having something. He knew I was interested in you. I'd been wanting to court you for years before the fight happened. It's my theory, now that I know you were infected with my virus, that my virus took action to infect you so you wouldn't be taken by another lycanthrope. Please believe me when I say I meant to go about courting you in a far nicer fashion, after I found a way to win you without costing you the career you'd wanted."

While I found that hard to believe, I decided I'd hear him out before judging him. "Why?"

"You were always something special. I've always believed if I won you, I'd never have to worry about breaking you. You were born tough. You could handle anything I tossed your way. You broke Brad's face with a crowbar, and you did it so it would hurt more. I've always thought you were incredible, but when you went after him to defend yourself, it confirmed what I'd always believed. You're vicious, but you're not malicious."

"Don't get your hopes up, Daniel. If I ever catch Brad alone in a dark alley, I'll be the living definition of malicious."

"If Brad knows what's good for him, he'll avoid you. If he even thinks of raising a hand against you, I'll tear him apart myself."

I frowned. Competing with Daniel for rights to beat the life out of Brad hadn't been part of my plans, such as they were. Then it filtered in that Daniel implied he would've infected me if given a chance. "And how would *you* have infected me?"

His answer would form the foundation of how I'd handle him in the future, if I needed a crowbar to rearrange his face, and how much effort I'd put into making a break for freedom.

His smile interested my virus too much for my own good. "My plan had been a simple but effective one. First, I'd convince you that I'm worth sticking around for. Then, after proper disclosure of the nuances of the lycanthropy virus, I would've begged you to marry me. Then I would've begun a very long campaign of making love to you repeatedly to ensure infection."

Daniel's blunt admission shocked me, revved my virus's engine, and added to my desire to break the extra bed to ensure maximum chances of giving him exactly what he wanted. "Oh."

Great. I sounded like an idiot.

"It would've taken me years to get through my plan. We owls have an almost ritualistic approach to courting. My mother thinks it's because you women want to make sure us men aren't useless wastes of air like Brad. It begins with food. An interested man, such as myself, will make food offerings to the woman he wants to court. If accepted, it's considered an invitation to make additional advances. It's a game. By offering you food, I'm displaying my interest. You, as the one I'm courting, will try to take me for all I'm worth. You'll ask for better food, things you want, or issue challenges. I need to prove I'm determined enough to earn the right to be your partner."

"Wait. You'll feed me, I'll ask for stuff, and you'll just give it to me?" I blurted. "How's that even fair?"

"If I succeed, it's generally accepted you'd be agreeing to be my mate. That's worth any challenge you throw my way."

I narrowed my eyes, well aware he'd bribed me with a lot of food to lure me to his hotel room. "And this started by your offers to feed me?"

"Until you're healthy, gaining weight, and settled, any food offerings are platonic in nature. I need to earn you. When you accept my offerings, you'll do so knowing exactly what you're getting into."

"I better still get those cupcakes. An entire box of them."

"Let's start with one. I'd rather you didn't get sick. When you're ready to tackle an entire box of them, I'll provide them as promised."

I couldn't argue with him since I didn't want to get sick, either. "I want beef jerky. You taunted me using your damned dog. I thought about eating your dog."

"That dog is actually my boss, a wolf lycanthrope with a potent illusionary ability. He was keeping an eye on Brad. Brad doesn't realize he's being monitored."

"Oh."

"I wasn't trying to taunt you. I had no idea you were starving."

"I'm not good at hunting," I whispered.

"It'll be better now," he promised. "I'll teach you everything you need to know, and those nights you don't catch anything, I'll make sure you go to bed with a full stomach anyway."

I couldn't remember what it felt like to be anything other than hungry, and once the first frustrated tear leaked out, I couldn't stop the rest from falling.

Chapter Three

SINCE OWLS COULDN'T CRY, I shifted, hid under the table, and hooted my shame over falling apart. My retreat didn't help; Daniel followed me, freeing me from the scraps of my ruined clothes.

"I'll take you shopping after you've gotten something to eat. While your cards should be ready by the end of the day, we'll worry about picking them up tomorrow to give you a break and a chance to get settled. In the meantime, we'll use mine, and I'll make sure your work is covered. I'll even take back everything I said about the cupcakes. You can get as sick on as many cupcakes as you want."

If I was going to get sick anyway, cupcakes would make it worthwhile—maybe.

"How does this sound? I'll get a bracer, I'll take you to my hotel, and then you can shift and get settled. You really need to let a CDC doctor have a look at you. I don't want you to get ill, and you probably will. You're stressed and hungry."

Fluffing my feathers at the idea I couldn't take care of myself, I stood on one foot and displayed my talons.

"Yes, you have pretty feet."

I hooted at him and clicked at his misinterpretation.

"I have no idea why you're annoyed."

At least he'd gotten that part right. I'd lost count of the reasons to be annoyed. If a CDC doctor poked at me, I really wouldn't be able to hide again. Minute by minute, my chances to disappear faded to nothing.

Daniel would hunt for me again, and I believed him to be persistent enough to find me.

"Are you worried about the doctor?"

With no other way to communicate with him, I settled my feathers, clacked my feet, and bobbed.

"The doctor isn't going to hurt you. You need a basic health exam and a virus scan. If you're sick, the scanner will pick it up. It'll also help let us know what you need in your diet. Everything will be all right. Once the doctor's done, you'll be able to eat and get some sleep. Within a week, you'll feel a lot better."

If he fed me for an entire week, it'd be a good thing I didn't own extra clothes; I'd balloon in weight and nothing would fit. When I hunted and caught something, a single meal reduced me to a near-comatose state. My virus wouldn't be happy with my inability to pursue its desires, but I'd grown used to its flighty nature.

For the moment, it wanted Daniel, but it would be disappointed if it thought I could be bought for a few cupcakes, steak, and lobster.

A knock at the door startled me into retreating from Daniel, and he twisted around to glare at the door. "It's open."

Miranda strode in carrying a leather brace. "This was the best I could find. It's for falcons, so try to convince your owl to keep your arm intact." The woman leaned over and peeked under the table. "Startled her into shifting again?"

"Something like that. Can you send a doctor, preferably a woman, to my hotel room?"

"Already ahead of you. She'll be there in twenty minutes. Head on over and take your lady with you. I also asked the doctor about what to feed her and sent someone to bring around everything you need. Sorry, Emily. No cupcakes for you today. The sugar will make you really sick."

Foiled. I fluttered my wings, poked my head out from beneath the table, and waited for Daniel to strap the leather bracer around his forearm. Once he seemed ready, I took flight and settled on the leather, careful to keep from digging my talons into his skin.

"Well, she's cooperating, and her general flight control is excellent. She's better at a floor takeoff than you are."

I preened at the compliment.

"She's not!" he protested.

Miranda pointed at the floor. "She is. She barely left a gouge in the hardwood."

Daniel stroked his hand over my head and back. "She's lightweight because she's starved."

"Relax, Mr. FBI. You can posture for her when she's better able to enjoy it. I'll tell the folks upstairs you're going to need the week to nurse her back to health, and I'll make sure Brad stays away while she's resting. The last thing we need is for you to lose your shit because you perceive a threat to her."

"I won't complain if you convince the CDC to send him packing for a while."

"No one would complain if the CDC encased the fucker in concrete and tossed him into the bay, either. But they won't because that's illegal." Miranda wrinkled her nose. "I'll compile a list of legal ways we could get rid of the fucker permanently."

"You're forgetting I'm an employee of the FBI *and* the CDC, Miranda."

"No, I'm not. I'm deliberately giving Emily ideas so should Brad go after her, breathe the same air she does, or otherwise provokes her in any fashion, she gets away with it. You could deal with a few months of community service, right?"

I could deal with a few years of prison for the satisfaction of picking pieces of Brad out of my claws. I hooted and bobbed my head.

"See? She likes the idea."

"Please stop encouraging her," Daniel begged.

"No, I don't think so. I want a proper wolf for Christmas, Danny. This year. And she's my best chance of getting one. I'll even get on my knees and beg."

I spread my wings, puffed my feathers, and clacked my beak at her.

Daniel bounced his arm beneath me. "Emily, she wants a proper *wolf* for Christmas. I'm an owl, remember? Just like you. She's not infringing on your territory. You get him out of here for the next few weeks, and we'll talk about getting you a proper wolf for Christmas. But it's going to cost you, especially if I lose my job because I ignored two women on a mission."

"You're joking, right? No one with a single grain of sense is going to get in the way of two scorned women on a mission. Just let us ladies do the real work and stay out of the way. We'll talk, Emily," Miranda promised. "I'll make sure the asshole is evicted from the state and given some hard labor to keep him busy while I do the legal footwork to see just what we can get away with. I'll stick around as long as I can, which shouldn't be too hard because your little lady is going to need a lot of legal advice to get back on her feet."

"Thanks, Miranda. I appreciate it."

"Just get her to your hotel room and settle her in before you bite someone. Also, remember the doctor needs to come into your room to care for her, so you can't be a territorial idiot today."

"Yes, ma'am."

"Good. Run on, now. I have calls to make and a case to build. And if you run into Brad, Emily? Tear his face off for me."

If Brad was stupid enough to come near me again, I would, and I wouldn't even care how long I spent in prison over it.

DANIEL'S HOTEL room was a two-bedroom suite. A doctor waited inside, a pretty red-haired woman too interested in him for my liking. At the rate I fluffed my feathers and spread my wings, I'd remain a ball of anger for the rest of my life. Clacking my beak didn't deter the woman, although her attention shifted mostly from him to me.

"Relax, Emily. Sorry, Annie. She's hungry and annoyed I've turned things upside down on her. How'd Miranda coerce you into coming over? I thought you were working the San Francisco circuit today."

"I got called in as soon as word got out you'd found her. Miranda warned everyone there was a cranky hybrid with an even crankier female in need of medical attention. The rest of the office fled in terror. I had six people volunteer to take over my shift, so here I am. I see she picked up your virus. She's a lot smaller than you are, though."

"She hasn't been able to eat much."

"And that explains the cooler of raw beef and chicken someone delivered five minutes ago. I'd told Miranda she'd want to feed her as a human; I'd missed the memo you were bringing her over as an owl. Feed her first. There's no point in running the scanners if she's going to try to take my hand off because she's hungry and I'm made of meat." Annie pointed at a cooler positioned next to the couch.

Daniel chuckled and headed over, sat down, and flipped it open. A treasure trove of bloody meat demanded my immediate attention, and I hopped off his bracer onto the edge of the cooler.

Even though the meat was sitting in a cooler, it was still warm. I hooted and snatched a piece, gulping it down before attacking the next morsel. No matter what, my stomach wouldn't stay empty for long.

"I was going to feed you," Daniel complained.

"Dan, when a woman's that hungry, your job is to provide the food and get the hell out of the way. How far undersized do you think she is?"

I liked the way the doctor thought, and I devoured as much as I could without choking on it. Within a few bites, my abused stomach bulged.

Daniel dared to stand up and dislodge me from my perch before dragging my cooler away. Hooting protests, I hopped after him. The bastard shunted the cooler outside and closed the door to keep me in and my dinner out. "You'll get sick. Digest for a few minutes, then you can have some more. Frankly, I'm impressed you didn't choke. Let Annie look you over in the meantime."

"Why don't you go find her a small treat, Dan? That way, I can get a better look at her, discuss her options, and get her settled. Take two hours. No coffee or foods with high caffeine, and try to limit the sugar to tolerable degrees. A *small* treat. I'll make sure she eats the appropriate amount while you're gone, and it'll give her a chance to relax without you hovering like a lunatic."

Daniel tensed. "But what if she runs?"

"Give me a break. She rode on your arm the entire way here. She has wings. She could've easily flown off. Look at her. She's cranky you rationed her food so she doesn't get sick, but she's remarkably patient and non-aggressive. Go find her something she'll enjoy. If she flies off, I'll accept responsibility. She doesn't need you hovering during her medical exam. Remember: *small* treat. Save your overtures for a better time."

Something turned Daniel's scent sharp and unpleasant, and he stormed out of the room spitting curses at Annie, who grinned at his departing back. He even slammed the door, startling me into hooting.

"Unmated lycanthrope males. So much drama. All right, Emily. Why don't you go into the bathroom and shift for me, then we can get this exam out of the way and have a talk about your situation. There's a bathrobe inside, and I'll take your sizes so we can get you some proper clothing."

I wanted to avoid the talking, but the lure of being a human again, a human who could eat and do the little things I'd missed for so long, goaded me into hopping to the bathroom, slipping inside, and shifting.

While shifting to an owl had suppressed my tears, the instant I returned to my human form, they spilled out. While I wanted to find somewhere to hide, Annie joined me in the bathroom, sighed, and grabbed the robe, slipping it over my shoulders. "Part of that is your virus, Emily. Just let it out.

Your virus has a life of its own, and it perceives safety and security in numbers. Since Dan has the same strain of virus, it's relieved. That translates into you becoming a sobbing mess with little provocation. Lycanthropes of any stripe don't do well alone. Add ready access to food, thrown in someone willing to make certain you don't starve again, and it's no surprise you're a mess. The first few times you eat as a human, you're going to get sick. That's going to alarm Dan because he's an invested lycanthrope male and that's what they do. He'll hover until it drives you insane, but there are advantages to him being around. He'll keep unwanted people away, and he'll give you a chance to rest and put on some weight."

I floundered, and Annie handed me a box of tissues. "I hate crying."

She grinned at me. "Considering how prideful I've been told you are, no surprise there. Don't sweat it. You'll keep Dan on his toes, which is exactly what he needs, and you need a man who is up for the challenge of handling you. A woman capable of hiding from a joint FBI-CDC task force is someone special. But, that said, you're not going to be caged, tested, or otherwise treated like a monster for having lycanthropy. You could've gone for help."

"I didn't want to be infected."

"I know. He told me what you'd wanted to study growing up. Well, there's good news for you. There are options. You don't have to give up everything because of your status as a lycanthrope. Sure, it'll be tough, but I hope you'll one day be able to fully accept what you are now. Dan'll help if you let him. He's invested, and he's not going to give you up without a fight. Your behavior around him has given him hope. I may as well be the bearer of bad news here, but he's loved you since he laid eyes on you."

The truth hurt. It always did. "He's in love with a memory, then."

"I disagree. If anything, he loves you even more than he did when you were in school. It takes a whole lot of woman to do what you've done. As far as lycanthropes go? Every unmated male in the country is going to want you when they find out you exist. You're elusive, smart, and can take care of yourself. And they're all turned on by pride. Pride is what gets them into squabbles with their mates, and mated lycanthropes love squabbling. That's why Dan's so touchy right now. Anyway, let's get the physical exam portion of this over with. Then we're going to alternate you between eating as an owl and having soup to get as many calories into you as possible so you can start the recovery process."

ANNIE TORTURED ME WITH FOOD. She started with a bowl of soup, mostly broth with a few token vegetables tossed in to make me feel better about the situation. Once I drank enough to please her, she insisted I shift and let me gorge on however much meat I could stuff down my throat. She repeated the process over and over until I emptied the entire cooler and counted my soup consumption in gallons.

She fed me straight into a dazed stupor, directed me to the nearest bed, and promised she'd stick around until Daniel returned.

I couldn't remember the last time I'd slept while someone watched over me. The last time I'd slept as I human, I'd awoken to smoke and fire, struggling to breathe. My home had burned, my skin scalded from the surging waves of heat the wildfire spewed as it devoured everything in its wake.

The terror of burning alive jolted me awake, and the dim memory of screaming haunted me. Warm hands cupped my face, and Daniel leaned towards me. "Emily, it was just a dream. Look at me," he ordered.

I fought to catch my breath, and I had no choice but to stare into his eyes. He pressed close, and my virus responded to him as always but in a new way. It settled and quieted, which made recomposing myself easier. The memory of facing my death still lingered, but his voice and firm but gentle touch offered sanctuary from the terror of the world burning around me.

"I can confirm your lungs are healthy. You have one hell of a scream. You all right?"

Instead of my home burning around me, a darkened hotel room enveloped me as much as Daniel's hands, caging me and reminding me I was human.

I sucked in a few deep breaths to steady my nerves. "Sorry. Just a dream," I whispered.

"Some dream. Most would call that a nightmare. I was about to slap you awake," he confessed.

Being slapped beat incineration any day of the week. "I'm fine now, really."

Without hunger constantly cramping my stomach, I could feel my heartbeat throbbing through me after having been startled awake. I ached in new ways, and the exhaustion I fought every day won more ground than usual. I rubbed my eyes, and Daniel lowered his hands and gave me space.

While I pretended I had control over the situation and continued composing myself, Daniel checked his phone. "It's about time to get up. I found a cupcake for you, and Annie even approved it."

"A cupcake for breakfast? Nice." Cupcakes beat nightmares, but if nightmares got me cupcakes, I wouldn't mind having them.

"The real breakfast Annie has planned for you isn't nearly as nice as my cupcake."

As I'd already gotten the lecture, I groaned. "More soup. Then she'll make me shift and gorge on meat. Then I'll have to eat even more soup."

"I'm afraid so. She wants your weight up yesterday, and that's the fastest way for a lycanthrope to gain weight. Next week, she'll add solid foods. Honestly, the only reason you're getting the cupcake is because I gave a wolf a run for his money in the whining department. She's tolerating it to keep me from annoying her."

"Heaven forbid we annoy the doctor. Pay up. I want my cupcake."

Daniel chuckled. "All right. I've been ordered to remind you this cupcake is not a part of my courtship efforts."

"Noted. It's going to cost you a lot more than a cupcake to trick me into anything, Mr. FBI."

He bowed his head. "Miranda's already teaching you bad habits."

"Is Mr. CDC more accurate?"

"Alas, I'm primarily employed by the FBI although I am an official employee of the CDC as well."

"You hate being called Mr. FBI, don't you?"

"Miranda does it because she knows it annoys me."

I smiled. "That sounds like an invitation to me."

"I can't win this no matter what I do, so you can call me whatever you want and I'll like it."

Banter and play beat fixating on my nightmare, and I forced myself to smile despite the lingering fear of burning to death. "That's good to know."

"What will the right to court you cost me?"

He asked a good question, one I didn't have the answer to. My virus had mostly given up hope I'd find a male I found tolerable. It wanted me to jump Daniel and get on with it, but I ignored its interest. "To begin with, tell me the full story about Miranda and that asshole."

He sighed. "There's not much to tell. He didn't disclose his status and talked her into sleeping with him. He got her drunk enough they had intercourse several times. He lied about using condoms on top of talking her into a blowjob or two. What she thought would be a fun bar pickup ended in infection and a mating bond with a man she hates. She's been with him ever since, hoping someone would off the bastard so she can find a new mate. Her virus won't let her kill him; she didn't realize what was happening until it was too late for her to act."

Brad had ruined my life, but he hadn't violated me in the same way. My fury rose, and for a rare change, my virus agreed with me. "That's my price."

"What?"

"That's my price. You help me off the bastard so Miranda's not trapped any longer."

"You're supposed to ask for food first."

Damn it. Were owls really that big of a pain in the ass? Then again, I operated on pure stubborn pride. I had no reason to doubt Daniel was any different. "Fine. I expect many culinary offerings from around the world. I'm not changing my mind about Brad, though. He took my life. He took hers. It's only fair for him to lose his. Even if there was a way to break the mating bond, he'd just infect someone else, wouldn't he?"

"Yes. That's part of why the CDC pays Miranda to put up

with the situation. They're trying to find a legal solution, but they can't justify killing him. If they do find some way to break the mating bond, he'd just move on to infect someone else. He could be imprisoned, but that wouldn't help Miranda. From my understanding of the situation, there are ways to break the bond, but it's damaging—more so than him being killed. So, they offer her monetary compensation until they can find a better solution."

I had a solution. The only question was if I could get away with it. "We kill him, but we do so in a way the FBI and CDC turns a blind eye. Can it be done, Mr. FBI?"

"I'll have to think about it. Maybe if I've gathered enough evidence he's violated his parole terms and put him in a situation he endangers someone, it might be feasible."

"Give me my cupcake and get to planning, Mr. FBI."

He obeyed.

Chapter Four

As expected, the cupcake induced a sugar high and crash I'd never forget, but it didn't tear through my stomach. All said and done, I called it my victory. My plans to execute Brad's brutal demise sat on the curb while I ate everything in sight and slept. The limited time I stayed awake between meals, I lounged in the tub while Annie or Daniel hovered.

Had I cared about my modesty, I would've been in trouble; Daniel got more than a few peeks when I forgot—or chose to ignore—he was in the room. I blamed my virus. It had ideas, ideas it wanted me to pursue. I had ideas, too, but impromptu naps tended to put a damper on them before I could do more than flash some skin.

I gave myself full points for holding his attention, as the more skin I flashed, the less likely he could be talked out of the room when Annie came to check in on me.

It took a full week for me to recover to Annie's satisfaction. When she left for good, I became the proud owner of a new driver's license and bank card along with a list of foods I should eat. A note next to cupcakes warned me against eating an entire box of them in one sitting.

According to the bank statement Annie had brought with her, in addition to the initial settlement, my unwanted infection won me three hundred thousand, and according to Miranda, he still owed me two hundred thousand. To my delight, she'd left me a copy of his parole terms.

The bastard served as the CDC's leashed dog, and he did whatever they wanted in exchange for not getting sent to prison. He took the high-risk jobs, and every cent of his hazard pay went to funding the settlement amount. To add to my sweet, sweet victory, the parole documentation listed the various types of jobs he had to do to remain out of prison.

I could live comfortably for years without worry of where I'd sleep, what I'd eat, or how I'd keep clothed. Restarting my life would take a chunk of the funds, but after working for over two years without spending hardly any of my earnings, I could go anywhere and do anything.

The real problem was Daniel, who dove head-first into my challenge to rid the Earth of Brad. A better woman would've found another way, one that didn't involve murder, but however much I liked the idea of Brad suffering a lifetime of debt and working as the CDC's dog, I worried for Miranda.

My virus's determination to secure Daniel as a mate writhed under my skin. I couldn't imagine what I would've done if my virus insisted on mating with someone I hated. Brad topped my short list of enemies. Were it not for Miranda, I might've been able to let go of the past, or at least satisfy myself with tormenting the bastard for life.

Vigilante justice might land me and Daniel in prison for a long time, but after weighing the pros and cons, I'd smile while burying the fucker and request Miranda visit from time to time.

My next obstacle was Daniel.

My virus appreciated him being close, but he hovered to the point I considered adding a second body to my to-do list. The only time he took his eyes off me was when I locked him out of the bathroom or Annie drove him off.

I needed to address his stalker tendencies sooner rather than later, especially if I wanted to return to work in a few days. Annie wanted me to wait until Thursday, believing the four extra days would add sufficient flesh to my bones and help me better adapt to a regular life.

I sat on the couch, grabbed the paperwork regarding Brad's parole and owed settlement, and slapped it against my leg. "Any luck devising a murder plan, Mr. FBI?"

"Yes and no," he replied, perching on the couch's arm, close enough to touch if I leaned a little.

"Elaborate."

"He has a bad enough record no one will put in a lot of effort looking for him should he disappear, but we'd be the primary suspects in a murder or kidnapping case. *If* an angel is requested, we'd face a premeditated murder charge. Miranda won't request one, but the judge might. It depends on a lot of factors, including the circumstances of his disappearance."

"How do we make him disappear without anyone looking for him or drawing attention to us?"

"We wait, bide our time, and catch him when he's supposed to be traveling. With a little magic, we can create an alibi only an angel would be able to see through."

I liked the sound of that. "What sort of magic? I don't have any practitioner skills."

"The same kind that tricked you into thinking my boss was a pet dog."

"Are you implying your boss would help us dispose of Brad?"

"I'm saying there's an entire line of people wanting to get rid of that low-life bastard. You and Miranda are at the front of it."

"And if everyone in line, excepting Miranda, joined forces to get rid of him? What are our odds of getting away with it?"

"Terrifyingly good if we make a solid plan and hide the body exceptionally well. We'll need to make certain suitable wolf candidates for Miranda are near her when we kill him, though. His death will hit her and her virus hard, and she'll need a strong pack to help her through it. We've talked about getting rid of him a few times."

I added find a good wolf for Miranda to my mental to-do list. "What stopped you?"

"Honestly, I'm not sure."

I considered all the options I had, most of which involved some form of landscaping machine. "We could run him through a mulcher, puree the mulched bits, and dump him into a river. He can feed the fish! If there's no body, no one can find it."

"Your *first* suggestion is to puree him?"

"What? It would simplify the problem of hiding the body."

"While truth, that's a little…" Daniel shrugged and held his hands up in surrender.

"Vicious? Brilliant?" I grinned at him.

"Gross."

"Don't you start with me, Daniel. We hack out balls of fur and bone after every meal. It's not a far leap to mulch Brad."

"Emily, you want to mulch him. That's a far leap. How are

we supposed to clean up the mess after we mulch him? The mulcher would contain a lot of evidence."

"I've been informed most of life's problems can be solved with the appropriate amount of gasoline and fire. We torch the mulcher, take it to a junkyard, crush it into a tiny cube, melt it down, and get paid by a scrapper for the raw metal."

Daniel's mouth dropped open.

"What? I thought it was a good idea. If we use a gas-powered mulcher at a field burn site, what we can't dump into the river is easy to hide, especially if we make a compost pile nearby contaminated with fragmented chicken bones. And cow bones. And pig bones. We could have a barbecue to celebrate."

His eyes widened, and he slowly lowered his hands. I waved my hand in front of his face, but his gaze remained locked on me. "We could drag a grill out to the site and turn it into a party. No one needs to know our bonfire has a mulcher in it. It could be a pyre! Would we need to dump him in the river if we burn him sufficiently?"

Daniel gulped. "Not to ruin your daydreaming, but the teeth and bone fragments would probably survive."

"We could dump those in a nearby river and make sure there's a lot of BBQ bones left at the site. Wouldn't that hide the evidence as long as we got rid of his teeth?" I stretched, propped my feet on the coffee table, and watched him through half-lidded eyes. "Admit it. You like the idea."

"Almost as much as I enjoyed watching you lacerate his face with your talons. I'm less concerned about getting any satisfaction out of him. I am concerned he'll come after you. He blames you for everything he's dealing with now. If a chance comes along, he'll attempt to get revenge. He's a sick bastard, and he might even try to violate his mating bond with Miranda to hurt you."

"He's the type," I agreed.

"He is."

"It'd be more criminal to leave him alive."

"I do believe you're right."

"We could lure him off a cliff and peck him to death. Lycanthropes can drown, can't they?"

"Where would we find a cliff tall enough for this plan?"

"Dover?"

"How, exactly, would we lure him to England?"

"Carefully. We could get Miranda to help. I'm sure she'd love to. It'd be a lot harder to stick his death on us if we lure him overseas. Hell, we could just dump him in the ocean. No one would miss an asshole like him."

"He does have parents, Emily."

"But would they actually miss him?"

Daniel sighed. "They're his parents. I'm sure they would miss him."

"Well, they did a shit job of raising the fucker."

"I won't argue with that."

"I still think using the mulcher is a good idea."

"You also think making a funeral pyre and hosting celebratory barbecue is a good idea, too. And I'm not sure I want to think about the trip to the metal scraper to hide the rest of the evidence."

"Killing the bastard is worth celebrating. I'll bring the marshmallows."

"Only the marshmallows? What happened to the rest of the barbecue?"

"That depends on how many people would come to his mulching."

"We'd need to hold a raffle for tickets."

"We could do a pot luck. I'll provide the grills, and we'll roast marshmallows on his pyre."

Daniel's brows rose. "That doesn't sound sanitary."

"Give me a break. I said I'd buy grills for the barbecue portion of the meal."

"And where do you propose we do this?"

I sulked. "Stop ruining my dreams of murder with your realism."

"My realism will keep you out of jail after accomplishing your dreams of murder. It'll be difficult to court you if you're in prison."

"You could join me in prison. We could share a cell."

"It doesn't work that way, Emily."

"Well, it should. Fine. Not getting caught is important. Who do you know that'll help us not get caught?"

"I'm going to have to call in a lot of favors and start a raffle," he muttered, shaking his head.

"And you'll have to provide a lot of meat for my grills. And cupcakes. An entire buffet table loaded with cupcakes. I think lobsters can be grilled, too. And I like mushrooms. We can grill mushrooms, can't we?"

"Yes on all counts. I'm viewing this as my formal challenge to earn the right to court you."

I considered him, narrowing my eyes and looking him over. If I listened to my virus, it was all but a done deal, and if it got its way, I'd be taking him to bed within the next five minutes if not sooner. Was a lifetime with Daniel worth a dead Brad?

I didn't even have to think about it.

"If this gets rid of that lowlife fucker and frees Miranda, consider your challenge accepted. Until he's gone, there's no point in getting on with the rest of my life. He ruined everything."

"I won't pretend I understand what it's like having the choice taken from me. I was born infected. I understood from an early age what to expect. Some doors close, but others open. You'll figure it out. I'll help you. Marrying me will open more doors for you, too. The FBI and CDC like partnering mates together. Local law enforcement usually separate hybrid pairs; they often need to spread out the firepower, so to speak."

"I don't think I'd be a good whatever you are."

"Maybe not, but you'd make an excellent resource for finding people who don't want to be found. I'm positive I can help you find a better job than mowing lawns."

I bristled. "Maybe I like mowing lawns."

"Well, if you do, we won't need to hire a landscaper, and I promise I'll pay better."

"I think you'd win that competition by default. Until you came along, I worked so I could wash my clothes and pretend I wasn't at a dead end." As always, my bitterness surged and tainted my tone.

"It gets better from here, Emily. If making certain Brad's never able to hurt you or anyone else is what you need to move on with your life, I'll make it happen for you."

I thought about it, but when all was said and done, there was only one way I could reply. "If we had an outdoor wedding, would a bonfire big enough to torch a mulcher be too much to ask for?"

"I think I can come up with something."

DANIEL INVITED his boss to our hotel room, and I feared we'd be arrested for planning Brad's murder without having a chance to actually kill him. Jacob Marley, in the prime of his life with bright blue eyes and a cheerful smile, seemed too young to be anyone's boss.

"It's always nice when a missing persons case has a happy ending. Daniel refused to believe you'd died in that wildfire. It's been one of my longer searches with a life at the end of the investigation. That said, don't disappear on him again. My wife'll take my balls for a trophy if we have to keep traveling trying to track you down."

I frowned. "Why? Why put in so much effort looking for *me*?"

Jacob pointed at Daniel. "We've learned when it comes to dedicated lycanthropes in bad situations, the wisest course of action is to help. He's a good operative, and by finding you, we remove his distractions. You're a victim deserving justice, but to get you that justice, we had to find you first."

"I told Daniel I'd marry him if we could torch Brad's mulched remains in a bonfire at our wedding."

"She's a direct one, isn't she?" Daniel's boss muttered.

"I appreciate not having to make any guesses. She's worked herself up to an outdoor wedding with a bonfire meant to incinerate Brad's mulched remains while otherwise destroying the evidence of wrongdoing. Her motivations do include helping Miranda."

"Moving beyond standard revenge is important."

As Daniel deserved some discomfort, I said, "I've been informed Daniel had, from an early age, intended to find some clever way to infect me with lycanthropy, so as such, he has potential stalker issues we should address. I view Brad's unfortunate loss of life and ultimate disappearance as penance for his stalker tendencies. I'm pretty sure he hovers outside of the bathroom door when I shower."

"He's probably hoping you'll invite him in. Lycanthrope ladies typically determine when their suitor may continue his advances. He's going to shadow you until you formally reject him or invite him to your bed. Ural owls are doubly tricky, as you'll likely remain semi-uninterested until you've accepted his offerings. Your species is more ritualistic than others, although I suspect Daniel will be more impatient than other Ural owls."

Daniel sighed. "My parents are going to be so disappointed in me, but it's true. I'm trying to uphold their standards for courting you. I think I've been doing okay on that front."

"I wish you the best of luck, Daniel." Jacob picked up the stack of Brad's parole papers and flipped through them. "Here's the deal. Brad's been past his third strike for a while now. It's been documented he's violated some terms of his parole. His state of residency bars the death penalty. As such, Miranda's stuck. We've tossed around the idea of issuing a kill bounty through the black markets, but the problem is with Miranda. She's been with him long enough the CDC is unwilling to cause her additional trauma. However, I will divulge a flag in his record: the CDC will not investigate any disappearances unless Miranda is the one to file the request. The FBI has been notified of the flag and have issued their approval as well. As long as no evidence of murder is uncovered, he'll be listed as missing and presumed dead. It's unusual, but Miranda's testimony would have warranted the death penalty if his state of residence permitted it. He's very careful to keep his residency the same. He's aware he's courting the death penalty if he moves. In law enforcement terms, lethal force may be used in case of any signs of aggression towards you or Miranda. Daniel, if you were to get into a fight with him over Emily, you'd face some community service but be able to maintain your badge. Expect a six month suspension to deal with community service. Since I'm an asshole and have connections, I may insist your community service time involve settling Emily and Miranda following Brad's death. It would be the best use of resources. In Miranda's case, you'd be responsible for finding an appropriate wolf to partner with her."

Daniel's grim smile promised he had no trouble facing a six-month suspension or community service. "How thin is the provocation line?"

"Emily would be justified in taking her temper out on him in almost any circumstance. You're not. Should Emily be attacked, as her prospective mate, you'd be cleared of wrongdoing."

"What classifies as allowable aggression?"

Aggression classified as allowable? I listened with interest.

"On his part, yours, or hers?"

"Let's go with all three to be on the safe side."

"Common sense applies. Unless he acts *or* verbally threatens Emily, you can't do anything. She can curse him out all day long, but he needs to act first. Name calling is allowed, threats aren't. That applies to both of you."

I snorted. "All I'd have to do is tell Brad he's a dickless coward to provoke him. He's so insecure about his masculinity he's incapable of ignoring criticism of his limp physique. If I wanted to goad him into attacking me, I'd just tell him he doesn't have kids because he fires blanks, and as such, there's no point in gelding him."

Both men grimaced.

"What? The way he acts, I bet it's true."

Daniel glared at me. "It may be true, but you don't have to say it."

"He's a dickless coward."

"Just don't geld him," he begged.

"Murder's okay but gelding isn't?" I glared at Daniel and his boss. "How is that even fair?"

"Be grateful murder isn't off the table, Miss Hall," Jacob replied.

"True. I suppose I can live with just murder."

"And a humane, quick death. It seems important I insist you two keep any attempts to free Miranda from his influence humane."

"Think she'll want to help?" I asked, unable to hide my grin. "She could be my bridesmaid of murder. That sounds much cooler than honor."

Daniel's boss dropped the parole papers onto the table and pinched the bridge of his nose. "For some reason, I think she'd be delighted."

I made a thoughtful sound in my throat. "Where are we going to find a preacher willing to oversee a marriage after a murder? That's going to be a problem. Does the preacher need to know about the murder?"

"Good luck, Dan. You're going to need it. I'll bring in a few folks who can help make this go smoothly. If there's going to be a murder, it'll be so well done cops will be trying to solve it a hundred years from now. Try to keep your woman partially contained through this. We still have to follow some rules despite having the leeway needed to pull this off."

Daniel grunted. "Why do people keep asking me to perform miracles?"

"I'm sure you can handle it with minimal whining. You're not a wolf, after all. If you were, you'd be allowed to whine."

"With all due respect, sir, you're an ass."

"But I'm a helpful ass willing to help you plan a murder. I expect a wedding invitation." Jacob headed for the door. "Oh, and Dan?"

"Sir?"

"Despite your current beliefs, you do have to work tomorrow. Don't be late."

Chapter Five

FOR THE FIRST time since the wildfire, I had everything I needed to be me again, including the authorization to return to mowing lawns and fixing machines, clothes I didn't have to wash after my shift, and a rental to take me where I needed to go. The rental annoyed me; after years of driving a large truck, the sporty car handled like a hummingbird on speed.

I considered it a miracle I made it to work without crashing.

With no need to arrive extra early, I showed up thirty minutes later than normal, which gave me plenty of time to prep the trucks and mowers before anyone else arrived.

Nothing screamed normality like work on a Tuesday morning.

"Nice car," my boss greeted from behind me. "I wasn't sure you'd be here today or if we'd have another one of those contractors again."

I retrieved Annie's medical clearance from my back pocket and waved it. "Freedom is sweet, I've been declared healthy, and the pest had to go back to work today. The car's a rental, and I'm just using it today."

I'd start petitioning for something a little saner and with fewer aspirations to be a bird. If I wanted to perform aerobatics, I'd shift.

"Who's on the rental?"

"The pest is the main renter, but I'm listed as a special note. It's in the glove box if you need to see it." Eager to be back to doing something familiar, I headed to the back to start my routine of preparing the mowers and trucks. My boss didn't ask to see the papers, opting to return to his office instead.

In the week I'd been gone, someone had cut corners, and while I did my best to prep Isham's mower, I bet it would pitch a fit by noon and spew black smoke as part of its death throes. Unless Isham coaxed the machine, which I doubted even on a good day, it'd likely seek out its revenge on its operator.

I hoped Isham survived.

I rocked back on my heels, thumping my wrench against my leg trying to figure out the best way to tell the boss his mower might last a week if he prayed, set up an altar, and otherwise beseeched the divine for a miracle. The quiet summoned my boss, who crossed his arms and frowned while I engaged the mower in a staring contest. "It's too quiet in here. Quiet means trouble."

I pointed my wrench at Isham's misbehaving machine. "This piece of shit is about done. If Isham's lucky, it'll last through to the end of the day."

"Why is it you always tell me things I don't want to hear?"

"I'm usually right, sir. That's why."

"Well, when it kicks the bucket, you'll fix it as always.

You've been saying that old mower is about to die for years. You're on spillover today, so your schedule's light at worst. I got the lazy louts to pick up extra yards until you're back into the swing of things."

"I was gone a week. It's not that hard to get back into the swing of things." I rolled my eyes, dumped the wrench into the tool box, and untethered the mower. "The parts you're going to need will cost you more than buying a new mower. If you put in an order now, you won't be short a mower for long. Even if you want it repaired, it might take weeks to get the parts in."

"You love ruining my mornings, don't you?"

"Hey, I kept it alive for years past its original expiration date. I bet Isham drinks because he's convinced this piece of shit is out to get him."

"Point taken. Any other bad news about my machines you want to give me?"

I glanced in the direction of the garage where the mulcher and other equipment lived. "Depends. How much does a mulcher cost?"

"Cute, Emily. There's nothing wrong with my wood chipper. It's a year old. I know you like playing with the machines, but don't concoct reasons to fiddle with them. I'll put an order in for the mower, you just leave my wood chipper alone."

"How about if I slightly customized it? It's gaudy."

"No."

"Flame decals count as customization."

"Why would you want to put flame decals on my wood chipper?"

"If it cost so much money I can't customize or fiddle with it, it needs some bling." Mostly, I wanted an excuse to poke at its innards and see how effective it would be at transforming a lycanthrope into gruesome mulch, but I wouldn't tell my boss that.

"Who gave you sugar this morning?"

I grinned. "I call him the pest. He loves when I call him the pest."

"I bet he does. This pest that gentleman who carted you off last week? He's got some nerve, that one. Just so you know, those CDC contractors are almost as much of a pain in the ass as you are."

"Did a good job, did they?"

"They're not as good with the machines as you are, but they weren't slackers. Go ahead and load your mower on Isham's truck. I'll tell him he has your spillover until he gets a new machine that won't try to kill him. Don't touch my wood chipper."

"Come on, boss. Let me add some decals. I'll also do the maintenance on all the machines until the new mower comes in."

"Fine, but no fiddling!"

A GOOD PERSON didn't plan a brutal murder, but a good personal also didn't steal another's freedom. What Brad had done to me paled in comparison to Miranda's living nightmare.

Before I'd shifted for the first time, my virus had often ruled, bringing change in its wake, directing my interest in men at its whim. Before Daniel had come sniffing around, it had liked any man it thought might serve as a good mate. Once it locked onto Daniel, it had changed its mind, fixating on him.

It no longer bothered me about every available man to cross my path. Its interest began and ended with the source of my infection, fringing on a base need so strong I could barely resist its desires.

Miranda's virus likely responded to Brad the way mine responded to Daniel. It wasn't the virus's fault it couldn't understand it desired a monster.

The virus lacked morality.

I lacked morality, too, which I supposed was why I'd resort to murder to free us both from Brad's shadow. Even if I got caught, I'd tell an angel the truth. The government refused to free Miranda from enslavement, so I would, and I didn't care how many hours of community service I worked or how many years in prison I faced.

I finished my rounds prepping the trucks and mowers, and I eyed Isham's mower, pondering if I trusted the damned thing enough to help with the extra yards being done. If I worked fast and brought the tool box with me, I held some faith I could make it last until noon.

"Hey, how many were on my roster for today?" I howled, hoping I wouldn't have to head into the building to talk to my boss.

Either he'd been lurking near the back or I'd shouted loud enough to wake the dead, but my boss made his appearance a few moments later. "Six. Why? You thinking about testing your luck with Isham's mower?"

"Unlike him, I can fix it if it breaks while I'm out. I'll just have to take the tools with me and hope it doesn't break until after noon."

"Try not to break my tools being stubborn."

I rolled my eyes. I'd broken a few tools over the years, but I couldn't be blamed; he'd purchased cheap shit. Cheap shit broke, and after listening to me rant about the piss-poor quality of his tools, he'd invested in some that could take a beating without noticing. "I think they'll be fine."

"Don't break my truck, either."

"Give this lecture to Isham. *He* breaks things. I fix what he breaks."

"And you fiddle with them because you can. *No fiddling.*"

"Sharpening the blades and giving the engine a tune-up is *not* fiddling."

"If it isn't broken, don't fix it."

"Maintenance is required if you don't want them breaking." I hauled Isham's mower to my truck, got it loaded, and put the tools in the cab to keep anyone from getting any ideas about taking them while I worked. "It's like you want to spend extra money hiring a regular mechanic."

"No, I just don't want to pay for parts I don't need yet. Your roster is in your truck."

I sighed, recognized I wouldn't be winning this argument anytime soon, and headed out to finish my rounds before Isham's mower committed a homicide-suicide. The damned thing spluttered on me half the time, and I could make a few guesses why my co-worker drank at nights.

The mower cost me an hour with its stubborn idiocy, but I finished my rounds without injury to myself and with the damned machine barely functioning.

Old habits died hard, and I plowed through lunch rather than taking a break so I'd have extra time with the boss's prized mulcher and its instruction manual. After, I'd satisfy my whining virus with some exposure to Daniel and let him solve the lunch and dinner problem.

If my virus had its way, Daniel would be stuck feeding me by hand for every meal, and once my hunger abated, it would inevitably get other ideas. In that, I understood Miranda. Like it or not, and fortunately, I did like it more than not, my virus craved Daniel's company. I enjoyed pushing his buttons and watching his reactions.

My virus influenced me, and it had no conception of what made Daniel a person. His virus sang to mine, mine sang to his, and we ultimately drew closer like magnets set to lock. Miranda's virus couldn't understand it slept with a monster, and it wouldn't stop tormenting her until he was gone from the picture.

For a while, I worried she'd suffer, but I believed her virus would find a new male to interest it, and after Brad, she'd have a choice in the matter.

It occurred to me there was one way I could help her without needing a mulcher to get rid of the bastard. Any smart lycanthrope would want a woman like Miranda for his mate. If I spread word to the local packs about Brad's choice to circumvent and force her choice of mate, what would happen? Would they, like me, want to act?

Where the hell would I find a pack of lycanthropes to ask?

The question distracted me all the way from my last job back to work.

I should've stopped for lunch, and I expected a scolding from Daniel, which would ultimately lead to a scolding from Annie. My stomach, already spoiled from ready access to food, growled its discontent. Hunger I swore I'd never endure again annoyed me into clacking my teeth.

Sometimes, I wondered what sort of idiot assumed I could act like an adult. Oh, right. Me.

Back at work, all was quiet, and my boss had left a note on his door that he was working a job for one of his richest clients.

I chuckled at the request for rescue if he didn't return by four. With no adult supervision to stop me, I raided the garage and wrangled equipment so I could get a better look at the mulcher. It would be several weeks before it saw heavy duty unless we got a call about a downed tree, but if we did, it would be ready.

My boss found me cleaning the machine after I'd done a full inspection of how it worked. He scowled. "You're already fiddling with it?"

"I'm not fiddling. I'm cleaning and doing a parts check." I was also checking the blades to determine if the machine could mince human bone. I suspected it could tear through rocks without thinking twice about it. A gravel cruncher might work better, but my boss wisely rented that monstrosity when he needed it or bought gravel from a supplier like a sane man. The mulcher would have to do, assuming I could get my hands on one. Using my boss's wouldn't work; he'd expose me as the culprit in a heartbeat, especially if he noticed anything wrong with the machine.

Running Brad through it would likely ensure the damned thing wouldn't run quite right ever again.

If I wanted to use a mulcher, I'd have to buy one or make one.

I eyed the machine, and to toy with my boss, I asked, "Pink decals?"

"Will pink decals keep you from tearing apart my wood chipper?"

"I'm going with yes but only because I want to see Isham's face when he needs to use pink equipment."

"When you decide you've had enough with someone's bullshit, you're a mean woman, Emily. What did Isham do this time?"

"One too many hell shifts and forcing me to be grateful for a rescue from the CDC."

"Dare I ask why the CDC wanted you for a week?"

I sighed, but as I saw no real way to avoid the subject, I shrugged and replied, "The guy responsible for my lycanthropy infection needs to pay his fines. The CDC wanted to do a diet evaluation, check my virus levels, and integrate me with more lycanthropes." I held up my thumb to signal everything was fine. "They even gave me an updated license if you need a copy."

"Bring it to my office before you leave. I'll be here late tonight. Will you be sticking around?"

I got the feeling he meant long-term. "For a while at least. It depends on the pest they keep flinging at me."

"Lycanthropes have a reputation, but you're not the type to wander off without a good reason. Bring that agent around. I'll give him a stern talking to, especially if he thinks he's stealing my mechanic."

"Am I paid enough to be a mechanic?"

"Stick around, and you will be."

A raise? My boss was bribing me to stay with a *raise*? I squealed and clapped my hands. "Condition: I get to fiddle with the mulcher."

"Condition: you get to fix Isham's mower."

"I'm going to need a lot of parts if you want that to happen. You'd be better off getting him a new one. I'm pretty sure his is possessed by the devil himself."

"You're going to need parts for the trucks anyway, so I'll pay you to junkyard dive for parts. I'll clear you schedule for the week and give you a good budget."

"It'd still be cheaper to buy him a new mower, and the new mower would be better on gas."

"You'll still need parts for the mowers that aren't possessed by the devil himself," my boss countered. "It's a good challenge for you and will keep you out of trouble until the replacement arrives. Isham's old mower can become a spare if you can purify the sin from it."

I eyed the piece of junk still loaded onto my truck. "I'm going to need a second raise if you want me to exorcise that thing. Anyway, how did I become a mechanic?"

"You came in early, got bored, and started maintaining the machines to blow time. One day, your truck broke down, you stole my tools, raided a junk yard after making off with the petty cash, and fixed it yourself. You only have yourself to blame for this promotion and general raise. I only have to call in a specialist when something is really wrong. I figure you'll pick up the extra mowing jobs during the busy season but will spend most of your time here handling maintenance and keeping things working in the background. When the machines don't break, everyone gets more real work done around here."

I pointed at the mower. "That thing needs to be retired, but I'll try to salvage it as a cranky spare in case another breaks."

"In the meantime, put your mower on Isham's truck in the mornings. If you can't get it running reliably, take it to the junk yard. If you really think it's a lost cause, I'll put in an order for two and have the next oldest machine turned into a spare."

"I can think of a few candidates. I'll pillage this one for the few parts that are still good and have the rest salvaged to help pay for truck parts."

My boss heaved a sigh, shook his head, and returned to his office.

THE INSTANT I returned to the hotel, making it only a few steps inside the lobby, Daniel pounced, caught me in his arms, and buried his face in my hair. My virus settled, content with his display. Unless I kept a close eye on him—and my feelings —I'd run a high risk of falling for him, too.

"You smell like grease." He laughed. "What did you do at work today? Dismantle your truck? I thought you'd come home smelling like grass."

Home was a funny word, one I hadn't used since the wild-fire, and it woke pain deep in my chest. To cover my dismay, I replied, "I fiddled with the boss's mulcher. I also convinced him to ditch a relic of a mower. He wants me to do more work on the machines, and I'll even get a raise."

When I hadn't been able to access my bank account, wages were like everything else in my life, a dangerous pipe dream of hope.

"There's plenty of work I can do in the area if working as a landscaping mechanic makes you happy. There's a few good colleges in the area, too. You wanted to be a nurse in high school."

Daniel remembered? I'd all but forgotten. The truth stung even more than the idea of having a home again. "Lycan-thropes can't be doctors or nurses."

"That's not true anymore. The laws were changed a few years ago. There are enough lycanthropes around now that they need doctors and nurses, and there are plenty of people willing to take the risk of having a talented lycanthrope working on them. You can become a nurse if you want, or you can choose to nurse broken machines and play nurse with me." To make it clear what he wanted, Daniel pulled away and waggled his eyebrows.

I gave credit where credit was due: Daniel had paid more attention than I thought possible, and he tried to lighten the burdens of my infection with his special brand of humor. "You remembered I wanted to be a nurse?"

"I remember everything about you, Emily. You used to dip your fries in milkshakes but only when you thought no one was watching. You don't like pizza, but you ate it anyway because you didn't want anyone making fun of you. You adore berries, but your friends would steal yours because they knew you wouldn't tell them no. And cupcakes? You'd do a lot more than crack Brad in the face with a crowbar for a cupcake. You liked almond clementine ones with raspberry frosting the best. And if I told you I've acquired a raspberry mascarpone cake just for you, would you accept the ring I've been holding onto ever since the day I realized you're the only one I want to be my wife and mate?"

I had two choices: I could laugh or cry.

In reality, I did a little of both. "When did you decide that?"

"We were thirteen, and you'd gotten into a fight at school because someone was picking on one of the other kids. My parents helped me pick it out so I'd shut up, and neither appreciated how expensive the one I wanted was. I've since paid them back." He chuckled and gave me a push towards the elevators. "They were holding it for me while I was traveling looking for you. It arrived yesterday."

It filtered in that he might've been serious about the ring and the cake. "There's really raspberry mascarpone cake?"

Ever since I'd discovered how well the berries and the cheese played with each other, I'd developed a fetish for cakes with those flavors.

"There is. I hired a baker to make you one when I couldn't find any within a hundred miles."

I couldn't imagine how much a custom cake cost. "But why?"

Daniel herded me into the elevator and pressed the button for our floor. "You deserve it, that's why. You deserve to enjoy life again, and I want to be the man who you enjoy it with every step of the way. We're meant to be, and I intend to work hard to prove that to you."

I believed him. He'd kill an old friend because I asked it of him. "You have nothing to prove, Daniel."

Even I could see that.

"You'll take my ring without the cake, then?"

"If there's no raspberry mascarpone cake in my immediate future, you might live to regret it. That cake better not be a lie."

He grinned at me. "I may be a lycanthrope male, but I'm not stupid enough to get between a woman and her cake."

THE CAKE WASN'T A LIE, and I began to drool the instant I spotted it displayed on the dresser. Plump raspberries covered the entire thing. A second box of equal size waited beside it, closed and hiding its secrets.

"What's in the other box?"

"An obscene number of cupcakes, several of which are also raspberry mascarpone. My plan is to feed you into a state of euphoric complacency, after which I'll attempt my proposal. I expect to be rejected. It took my father three years of daily food bribes and proposals to convince my mother to marry him."

If Daniel's father was anything like him, his mother was insane for resisting him for so long.

"That would be a lot of cake. I'm not sure I could eat an entire cake and a box of cupcakes every day for three years."

"It's my job to vary my offerings for your enjoyment."

I licked my lips and contemplated how best to approach devouring the entire cake, which would likely lead to misery and regret later. I didn't care.

He'd gotten me an entire raspberry mascarpone cake, and I meant to enjoy every bite of it.

However, I also recognized if I didn't rein him in, I'd be eating entire cakes for dinner until I agreed to marry him. "I'll be expecting a lifetime of small treats. A cupcake is a small treat. That said, I think you're confused. Marrying you is a base requirement for our plan to rid the Earth of Brad. If I don't marry you, there's no wedding, and if there's no wedding, there's no murder. I'll accept future culinary bribes, but they're not actually necessary." I considered that. "Mostly. I'll expect at least one raspberry mascarpone cake a year."

There. I could have my cake and remove Daniel's ridiculous requirements to feed me into oblivion.

"You're supposed to make this difficult on me."

"I am. You have to wait until the wedding night for what you really want. No dead-beat Brad in a casket, no wedding night. I fully intend to enjoy this cake, and I'll even pretend I'm surprised when you propose and show me the ring."

"You don't need to act surprised. I'm just worried you won't like it."

"Let me guess: you've been worried about this since we were thirteen."

"Sounds about right."

"Ring first, then cake. And I'll be expecting you to feed me every bite."

"You're definitely an owl," he complained. "Only an owl would be so evil."

I allowed myself a smile. "If we're both intolerably frustrated, we'll work together to kill Brad faster."

"Have I ever told you I love how viciously dedicated you are?"

"Not particularly."

"Well, I do."

One of us was crazy. I just wasn't sure who.

AT THIRTEEN, Daniel had understood more about women—or at least me—than far older men. Other women might turn their nose up at the brown diamond, but I adored its shifting colors and endless possibilities. I'd forgotten how much of my childhood I'd spent chasing after impossible dreams.

The unknown had fascinated me.

"Do you like it?"

So many hopes and dreams hung on his question and my answer. A thousand little truths and shifts in my perspective transformed me more than my virus had. The ring and its single, precious stone meant more than what he'd paid for it so long ago.

Once upon a time, I'd complained about clear quartz for holding no surprises. I'd felt the same about diamonds.

In the depths of the solitaire, while it wasn't a large store, were a sea of endless colors and possibilities.

Even then, he'd listened to me.

"It's beautiful." As he feared, it didn't fit; it wouldn't

without a jeweler's intervention, although at the rate Daniel kept feeding me, I'd have to have the ring adjusted once a week.

If he kept aiming his most brilliant smile in my direction, I'd go blind. "Really?"

"I never liked clear stones."

"I remember. You couldn't stand how you could see right through them. No depth. No mystery. I wanted to give you a mystery you could wear, but I wanted it to be something meant to last, so I wanted a diamond."

No wonder he'd driven his parents to the brink of sanity while attacking their wallets. "You succeeded."

"I hope you realize feeding you every bite of that cake is going to test my restraint and resolve, right?"

I set the ring back in its box on the dresser. "You told me to test you, so I am. You know my demands. Please don't disappoint me—and let me help."

"Let you *help*? Are you kidding? I'm going to watch and help you dispose of the body. Oh, and plan the wedding. How does me handling planning the wedding while you commit the murder sound? Does two months from today sound good to you?"

Was two months enough to plan a murder? I hoped so. "Sure."

"Excellent. Now, how about some cake?"

Did he really think I'd say no?

Chapter Six

THERE WERE two types of murder: spontaneous and premeditated. Most premeditated murders only included a few—if any—accomplices. In a twist of fate, or perhaps a sign Brad was even filthier than I believed, we had an entire army of people willing to help me on my mission to set Miranda free from the scumbag lycanthrope.

It hadn't taken me long to find four suitable wolf suitors eager to help her pick up the pieces following his death. I'd lost count of the number of interested lycanthropes, but only six had fit Miranda's wish list for a perfect man, and something about two of them rubbed me the wrong way. Daniel thought something was off about them, too, which made it easier to cut them from the list.

To expose them to Miranda, I suggested Daniel add them to his wedding party. I'd make Miranda my bridesmaid-of-murder and let nature run its course. To throw them together as often as possible, I turned into a bridezilla who demanded frequent outings to restaurants.

Unlike other bridezillas, I paid for everything, dipping into the money I had earned over the years. Daniel sulked, but he recognized I needed to pay my own way so he only gave me a little trouble in the evenings when trying to come up with his latest treat to keep my interested focused solely on him.

I enjoyed the game almost as much as the cupcakes and other treats he provided.

I began my planning with the help of the six cops who were willing to give theoretical advice on how to make bodies disappear with little hope of recovery. To my delight, mulching the slimy bastard, lighting him on fire, breaking the machine into a million little pieces, and dumping the remains in a remote place stood a strong chance of working.

Brad's bones and teeth would go into the rapids a mile from the wedding site, a location only Daniel and a chosen few knew. Miranda had the job of luring Brad to the site. My job was to show up in a pretty dress, accept the crowbar Daniel offered me, one he'd painted white and decorated with ribbons, enjoy the mayhem, murder, and general festivities, and leave happily married to Daniel.

I kept getting stuck on the happily married to Daniel part of things. My virus adored him. He walked into the room, and it calmed, quieted, and basked in the glow of his presence. I should've resented him for his part in transforming me into a lycanthrope, but my hatred had already run its course and focused on the one man who'd been truly guilty of the crime.

Day by day, my resentment melted away, and if not for Miranda, I might've even been willing to forgive Brad for his role in changing my life.

My virus understood what I was growing to accept: for better or worse, Brad's actions had paved the way for Daniel to become a serious part of my life, and he wouldn't have had to battle my dreams of becoming a nurse before the laws had changed.

I'd had a chance to see life without him in it, and the longer I spent with him, the more I wanted him as a constant, a fixture in my life I could rely upon when I got tired of fighting all the time.

Without Brad's interference, I might've remained stuck with the resentment of losing my childhood dreams.

To prove I could become anything I wanted despite being infected with lycanthropy, Daniel went out of his way to find schools with night courses, and some of them openly admitted lycanthropes to their classes, specializing in treating those with the infection.

He'd told me the truth.

I could pick up the pieces I thought broken beyond reclamation if I wanted. I could also choose to stick with doctoring cranky mowers and other landscaping equipment. Some doors had closed, but others had opened, and some I might be able to open again with some work.

It left me with a lot to think about.

A week after returning to work and confirming I'd marry him at a time, date, and location of Daniel's choosing, I took the initiative to find an apartment for us on a month-to-month lease. Then, once I had the keys in hand, I invited Daniel into my domain.

Sharing a bed with him tested my patience, gave my virus ideas, and drove Daniel crazy. According to my nose, the instant we escaped our wedding ceremony and reception, I'd learn a lot about what happened when an eager lycanthrope finally got let off his leash.

I doubted my poor wedding dress would survive.

As I had rather bloody plans, I actually had three wedding

dresses: one to wear when I took my white, ribbon-wrapped crowbar to Brad's face and beat him until he'd never bother anyone again, one to marry Daniel in, and one for the reception.

For some reason, everyone expected me to ruin all three dresses, so there was even a forth one kicking around somewhere, but from my understanding of the situation, the only one who'd see me in it was Daniel, I'd wear it only long enough for him to take me out of it, and it would probably die a terrible death like the others. I found the whole thing puzzling, but Miranda had made the mistake of mentioning the fourth dress's absurd amount of lace, capturing Daniel's undivided attention.

A week before the wedding, Daniel ditched work and followed me around like a lovesick puppy. According to Jacob, until we were safely mated, I'd have a living shadow determined to keep other males away.

I wondered what my boss would think of the pest loitering around while I worked.

I didn't have to wait long. Within five minutes of arriving, he made his appearance, looking over Daniel from head to toe. "I see you haven't ditched the pest yet, Emily."

I rolled my eyes and started my check of the mowers. "I already told you I'm taking two weeks off starting Friday. To marry the pest. And do whatever it is newly married people do with two weeks off work."

"We're going on a honeymoon," Daniel reminded me. "We're going to Europe. You even got your passport expedited so we would go."

"I'd agreed to let you plan the wedding. I didn't sign any contract about some two-week whats-it to Europe."

"Honeymoon."

"We're not wolves. I have no interest in moons." I poked and prodded at the first mower in the lineup to cover my smirk. "I don't mind honey, though."

"If it contains sugar, you'll do everything short of selling your soul to the devil," Daniel muttered.

"I haven't married you yet," I countered.

"Are you saying I'm the devil?"

"I'm saying I've never seen you and the devil in the same place before."

"Have you even seen the devil?"

I shrugged. "My point still stands."

"I can't tell if you like him or hate him," my boss muttered.

"He can't, either." I grinned and stopped goofing off so I could have everything done before the rest of my co-workers arrived. "And you can't run any of the machines over him, Pete. I like this specific lycanthrope. I've been informed he's going to be addled and follow me around until I actually marry him, so he's going to be puttering around here getting in the way all week."

"Leash him in a corner if he gets in the way."

"He's not a wolf. He doesn't need to be leashed." A cage might work, if I could find one big enough for an owl his size. He'd shifted for me several times, and I had a lot of growing to do to catch up. On the other hand, I enjoyed being able to hide under his wing at my leisure.

"I figured not. You'd eat a poor wolf alive. You're far too solitary to be a wolf. You also don't whine."

Daniel chuckled. "She's a lot flightier than a wolf."

I scowled. "That comment supports my certainty I've never seen you or the devil in the same room together."

"Admit it, Emily. You appreciate my refined sense of humor."

"Refined? You're punning me." The bastard was even punning me using our species in front of my boss.

I wanted to believe only death would do, but death was too merciful of a fate for him. No, I'd spend the rest of our lives working on suitable payback.

"You're just happy because you know owl be yours forever."

"You're really the devil. You're not going to hell. You run the place. That was awful."

Daniel grinned at me. "Admit it, Emily. You like it. You also like knowing I've already ordered something special for us for dinner tonight. I even accounted for the time needed to head home so you can pretty yourself for our outing."

I needed to have a long talk with my stomach and its inability to resist Daniel's offerings. I also needed to have a long talk with him about his belief I could be prettied up without anything short of gargantuan effort. "We're going out tonight?"

"We are."

That was new, and I eyed him, wondering what he was planning. "Do I still get my cupcake?"

"You'll enjoy your dessert as usual, never fear. I'm afraid you'll have to accept something a bit more decadent than a cupcake, however."

I licked my lips. "You have my attention."

"I'd like to keep your attention when you're not working," he replied, his amusement warming his voice. "I even have plans for lunch, too, as you have a bad habit of forgetting to feed yourself."

My face flushed that he'd figured out I kept skipping lunch.

"Well, at least I don't have to educate you on her eating

habits," my boss announced. "That leaves me with the standard lecture."

Daniel frowned. "What standard lecture?"

"You hurt my mechanic, and I'll make sure you live to regret it. I don't need to be a lycanthrope to make you suffer, boy. I figure I can recruit a few extra hands to deal with you as needed."

I covered my mouth so I wouldn't crack up laughing at the thought of my boss putting Daniel in his place. Rolling my eyes over the men about to start displaying like peacocks, I focused on my work to avoid the embarrassment of them bickering over me.

"The last thing I want is to hurt her."

"Well, someone did, and it took her months before she stopped flinching around the boys. You make her flinch, and I'll teach you just how much damage an industrial lawn mower can do to someone."

"His name's Brad," Daniel replied. "If he has a single brain cell left in his thick skull, he won't bother her again."

I admired how Daniel skirted the truth, and I shook my head over his willingness to identify the asshole who'd ruined so much of my life.

"Why don't we go have a talk in my office, son? You stick around here while she's prepping the mowers, and she'll be too busy sneaking peeks to work, then she'll get mad because we distracted her, and trust me when I say only a fool distracts her when she's on a schedule."

Great. I gave it five minutes before they were gossiping in my boss's office. At a loss of how to stop them, I shook my head and got to work so I could get on with the rest of my day.

My boss kept Daniel busy until lunch, something I considered a miracle, but if I had my way, I'd keep tearing apart the backhoe determined to discover why the damned thing kept stuttering instead of turning over. Once the engine started, it ran like a champ, but getting it to work involved some teeth grinding, prayer for divine intervention, and a shameful number of threats.

I suspected the spark plugs were to blame, but I worried some other gremlin infected the machine.

Daniel tapped his foot and crossed his arms. "Step away from the big machine, Emily. It's time for us to go to lunch."

I twisted around to glare at him. "It's still broken."

"It won't be going anywhere while we're having lunch."

"But it's still broken."

"Emily, leave it. It's lunch time, and you need food."

"But I'm not done here."

Daniel strode over, and I hissed at him. He ignored me, wrapped his arm around my waist, and lifted me off the floor. I grabbed for the backhoe's door and held on. "I'm not done!" I howled.

I clung to the backhoe, he pulled, and my knuckles turned white from the effort of keeping him from dragging me away from my work.

"Why are you being stubborn? I'm trying to feed you. You have to leave for me to feed you. I have plans, and they involve us leaving for an hour."

"But I'm not done here."

"Emily, we're going to lunch. It'll be here when we get back." Daniel grunted and pulled harder until my fingers slipped and I lost my hold on the backhoe. He dragged me towards the door while I scrambled for a handhold. "No wonder you got away with so much. You're determined. You need lunch, and you need lunch now."

"I wasn't done working, damn it!"

My boss chuckled. "This explains a few things. Emily, no one will touch the backhoe. It's definitely not going anywhere with parts of its engine dismantled. Just put it back together when you get back."

"I need spark plugs."

"Have your man take you to pick up the plugs after lunch. Use lunch as an excuse to go pick up parts. Just bring me the receipt so I can comp you for any expenses."

Without noticing my weight or struggling, Daniel hauled me to the door. "I'll take her to get the parts she needs. Anything else while we're out?"

"Get her something she likes to drink to put in the fridge. Try to get her to drink something other than water for a change, even if it's that sparkling crap."

Daniel sighed. "I'll bring something for her."

"Hey, I like water just fine, thank you!" I'd spent years guzzling water. I liked it. Water was life, and I wouldn't betray it.

"When your boss says to get you something for the fridge, I'm getting you something for the fridge. I'll bring her back in an hour."

"Take as long as you need in the parts store. They have a section dedicated to decals. Let her loose and point at the most feminine ones you can find. She's been on a mission to trick out a few of the machines. If she tries to get parts for the wood chipper, please try to stop her."

"Really, Emily?" Daniel laughed, shook his head, and

dragged me towards his rental. "I'll try to keep her partially contained, sir."

"You do that. I wish you the best of luck. You'll need it. I'll be in my office if you need me, so just give a call."

Daniel refused to let me go until I surrendered and buckled in. He even closed the door and waggled his finger at me as though it might actually keep me in the vehicle. It did. I couldn't bring myself to spoil his efforts to drag me away from work.

Through it all, my virus slept, everything perfect in its little world.

Chapter Seven

I SPENT the week working on the mowers and making sure they would survive two weeks without any tender, loving care from me. Daniel spent more time with my boss than with me, which I found amusing.

Them becoming friends had been the last thing I'd expected, but I liked the development. I suspected Daniel reassured himself I worked for someone he liked and could trust. I'd heard about lycanthropes being overly protective, but it hadn't occurred to me that it would apply to every element of my life.

The novelty of being wanted kept me quiet, and Daniel's enjoyment of joining me at work ensured I waited around for him in the morning even when he made me later than I liked.

When Friday morning rolled around, I arrived to find every truck and mower already gone and a pile of gift-wrapped packages inside the garage along with a note consisting of two words: go home.

I crossed my arms and tapped my foot. "They took my mowers and left presents?"

"How terrible, your co-workers wishing you well the night before your wedding." Daniel counted boxes. "Twenty presents, all of them just for you. Whatever will you do?"

It'd been so long since I'd gotten presents from anyone I needed to fight the urge to pounce the pile and start tearing off the wrapping paper. Someone had even used cheery green and red Christmas paper on one of them. "This is when I'm supposed to hoard them like a dragon and hit anyone who tries to take them, right? Do I get to open them today or do I have to wait until tomorrow?"

"They're your presents. You can open them whenever you want."

While tempted to tear into them, I snatched Daniel's keys out of his hands and ran to the car to bring it closer so I could load my prizes before they grew feet and walked off.

His laughter followed me.

Once I had the car in place, I popped the trunk and began loading them in, giggling when I ran out of space and had to pile the rest on the backseat. Once done, I made sure everything was locked up so nothing would be disturbed while everyone was working. "No one told me I got presents for marrying you."

"It's traditional. Technically, they're presents for us, but I'm assuming they're all meant for you since your co-workers just glare at me like I'm a threat to their general well-being. I even promised I'd bring you back after our honeymoon. Maybe they're bribing you to stick around even if you decide to go back to nursing school?"

"Maybe if you'd stop strutting like a peacock and acting like they're threats to your future marital status, they wouldn't glare at you. And anyway, half of them are accident prone and it wouldn't hurt having someone who actually knows what they're doing putting them back together." I checked to make sure none of my presents would fall on our way back to our apartment and tossed his keys back to him. "Take us home. I have presents to unwrap."

Daniel laughed. "If I'd known how excited you'd get over unwrapping presents, I would've wrapped your cakes and cupcakes so you could enjoy them even more."

Blushing, I got into the rental and tried to ignore the reasons why so many presents excited me. "That sounds like a recipe for cupcake disaster. Ruined cupcakes would not be good, Daniel."

"This is true. You looked ready to cry when some of your raspberries escaped from your cake. I'm still concerned you're going to pick up some sort of illness from eating raspberries off the floor." He chuckled, waited for me to buckle in, and headed back for our apartment. "You'll appreciate the extra day off work tomorrow. We can relax, make certain we have everything ready, and double-check our plans."

"I don't have a mulcher. Every time I tried to get a mulcher, you kept refusing to take me to the store. You won't even take me to the junkyard. You keep distracting me every time I try to go."

His distractions had ranged from outings to restaurants, one venture to a farmer's market, a trip to the mountains for a hike and an evening flight coupled with a hunting lesson, and more cupcakes than I could shake a stick at. It was fortunate lycanthropes had wonky metabolisms; at my current rate of cupcake consumption, I should've gained at least a hundred pounds and diabetes.

"The type of wood chipper you want costs eight thousand at minimum. The model you like is sixteen thousand. You want to spend that much to use it once and light it on fire.

You refused to entertain a used or lesser model. As such, we have come up with several alternatives."

I scowled. "Like what?"

"It's a surprise. Consider it a wedding present from me to you. You'll even like it."

I would? "Will it be as satisfying as stuffing his deceased ass into a mulcher?"

"I'm hoping you'll like it that much."

I wasn't sure anything could top the satisfaction of making Brad disappear forever, but I'd trust his word—and accept I could spend the eight to sixteen thousand on something else. "You just didn't want me to spend that much money on Brad."

He chuckled. "That was definitely a factor. I also don't want to have to lug a charred wood chipper to a junk yard to be scrapped. It'd be awkward explaining why the wood chipper was charred. That sort of thing makes people ask questions. For the record, I tested to see how hard one was to clean after running a chicken through it. It was not pretty, Emily. It took three of us five hours to get it back into working order again."

"You ran a chicken through a mulcher?"

"It wasn't pretty. I will give you credit: you'd come up with a very good method of trashing the body, but upon closer investigation, it would be exceptionally difficult to remove all evidence."

I frowned. "Why?"

"You didn't account for the spray radius. There'd be evidence left everywhere, and while we could rig a controlled bonfire with some help with magic, we wouldn't be able to torch a sufficient space to completely remove the evidence. Also, don't ask about the smell or how far away we found bits of chicken."

Gross. "Point taken. So the mulcher plan is officially dead?"

"Unfortunately. I was volunteered to talk about the other options we have."

"We suck at premeditated murder, don't we?"

"I wouldn't say we suck at it. We're just being realistic and careful about our plans. We *do* have rules we have to play by. There's just too much risk of long-term consequences using a wood chipper. *If* you got away with it, it would be brilliant, but too much can go wrong."

"That is pretty disappointing."

"It was a horror show, Emily. When the wolves are horrified by the carnage, it's time to come up with a new plan."

I huffed. "Wussy wolves. No one was asking them to stuff the bastard into the mulcher. I'd do it myself."

"Do you know how long it takes to get blood out of your hair?"

"Well, no. I don't. I try to keep blood out of my hair in the first place."

"You would be covered head to toe in bits of Brad. He would get into your hair, into your clothes, and you'd be wearing him for the rest of the day. I don't want my wife to be wearing bits of Brad on our wedding day."

I considered that, grimacing at the thought of having to brush bits of Brad out of my hair. I also didn't want to think about where his bits might infiltrate in liquefied form. "You're possibly convincing me to avoid mulching him. Was the blood spray from the chicken that bad?"

"It was like a pillow factory exploded and took out a blood bank when it went. We were all rather impressed by the spray radius. Chickens have substantially less blood than humans. We weren't expecting the blood to spray out of every moving part in the machine, though. You don't want to know how hard it was to clean up. We had to return the damned thing in pristine condition."

I winced. "Okay, having done full cleanings of those machines, I can understand why that would not be fun. You used an industrial model?"

"I managed to get a hold of your dream machine for the experiment, and I paid a rather substantial price to do it. Someone had one they were willing to risk. He was confident a chicken wouldn't damage the machine, and when Jacob opened his mouth and told the guy you fixed these machines for a living, he seemed eager to give me a taste of what it was like having to tear apart one and properly take care of it. I've been educated. It wasn't nearly as easy as I thought it would be."

I giggled. "That's great. How'd you like pretending you're a mechanic?"

"I have a great deal more respect for what you deal with than I did last week. I had no idea how difficult it could get to make all those parts fit back together and work when done. We ultimately had to ask for help to get it back together again. And you learned how to do this from fiddling?"

Yep, Daniel had been talking to my boss a lot. "I'm not *fiddling*."

"You fiddle, Emily. You tear things apart to see how they work when you get bored. It's going to be my life's mission to make sure you never get bored. I'm concerned you'll dismantle the house if I let you get bored."

I thought about it, accepted he was likely right, and grinned. "You still have a chance to run away if you can't handle it."

My virus rejected my idea, and it writhed under my skin.

"I'm looking forward to handling you."

Nice. My virus liked the idea of him handling me, too. "Tomorrow, over Brad's dead body. Well, later that night because that's creepier than even I'm okay with. I draw the line at mulching his corpse."

"I'm so grateful you have a line, even though your line is still messy and disturbing."

"But satisfying."

"I can't argue with that."

MY CO-WORKERS HAD a twisted sense of humor. Every present included at least one item meant entirely for Daniel's enjoyment, and some of them were made of nothing but string barely held together with scraps of lace. I held up one such piece, both my brows raised high. "Should I be disturbed?"

"You can blame Miranda and Annie. Upon questioning, there was nothing in the doctor and bridesmaid-of-murder agreements barring them from sharing your clothing sizes with interested parties for purposes of showering you with gifts." Daniel's smile promised he meant to enjoy the scraps of fabric masquerading as clothing. "I find it amusing you're fixated on the lingerie when you have some really nice presents obviously meant for just you."

I bit my lip, dropping the latest piece of lingerie onto the pile and gave the other gifts my full attention. A fortune worth of tools littered the living room floor, someone had determined I really needed a black leather jacket in my life, a pair of ass-kicker boots in white, likely meant to be worn with my wedding dress for my date with beating Brad into the afterlife, a matching pair in black, more pots and pans than I knew what to do with, and a gift certificate to an auto parts store.

The gift certificate puzzled me, and I snatched it, waving it at Daniel. "This one is just wrong. I don't have a car."

Daniel made a thoughtful noise. "Oh. You don't?"

I shot him a glare. "You know I don't. You don't, either. You have an FBI-issued vehicle they gave you earlier this week to use for work. I think they feel sorry for you."

"Or they just got tired of paying for a rental."

"That, too."

"You're right. You don't have a car."

"Are all owls jerks?"

"Yes, we are." Daniel hopped to his feet, dodged the mess of wrapping paper and gifts, and headed into the bedroom. He emerged with a gold-wrapped box, which he tossed to me. "I was going to give that to you as a consolation prize for marrying me, but I figure you can use that as part of the festivities tomorrow."

"Was I supposed to get you a present? I didn't get you a present, Daniel."

"You are the present, and I'm completely happy with that."

"I'm not sure that's how it's supposed to work."

"We're owls. That's how it's supposed to work."

I rolled my eyes at his favorite method of tricking me into going with what he wanted. "You're shameless."

"I'm an owl. We defined what it means to be shameless."

"Keep telling yourself that, Daniel." I tore into the paper, found a small box within covered in duct tape, and waged a bitter war to gain entry to my prize.

Another box wrapped in clear tape waited inside. If his goal was to keep my attention and ensure I spent the rest of my life obtaining my revenge, he succeeded marvelously. "I should be grateful you didn't pull this shit where people might see me fighting with this tape."

"That had occurred to me *after* I'd finished wrapping it."

"This better not attack me."

"Nothing inside will attack you."

I didn't believe him, but if I wanted to find out what was inside, I needed to accept the dangers of opening a potentially sabotaged present. The first glint of trouble made its appearance after I defeated the first layer of tape. "I'm not cleaning the glitter out of the carpet."

"But it's edible glitter and sugar."

Fuck. "You either like ants or you felt the need to demonstrate your capacity for being an asshole."

"I also enjoy watching you try to figure out how to eat the delicious treat I've placed inside that box as a booby trap. Now that you know it's edible, you're going to be less likely to want to spill any of it. I'll be amused for hours while you try to get that open without wasting food."

"You, sir, are a jerk."

Daniel grinned at me. "But I'm a jerk who gives you what you need."

"In what universe did I need a box full of edible glitter and sugar?"

"This one."

I grabbed my new pot and pan set, tore into it, and retrieved the largest pot possible. To make it clear he wouldn't thwart me, I cleaned it, made certain it was completely dry, and went to work retrieving my prize and preserving the sugar and glitter for later use.

Within twenty minutes, I questioned how such a small box could contain so much sugar and glitter. I glared at the mess in the pot, wondering what I'd do with so much sugar and edible glitter. Inside, another box awaited my attention, but unlike the others, it was only held together with a few strips of ribbon and a tiny bow.

"Your expression is priceless."

Was it? I grabbed the box and eyed it. "Is this going to spill more food on me when I open it?"

"No. It's the real deal. I'm impressed you were so determined to save some sugar and edible glitter you used your new pot, though."

I flipped him my middle finger. "I will find something to do with this glittery sugar."

"I have no doubt about that."

After making sure I'd gotten all the glitter and sugar off the box, I tugged at the ribbon, discarded it and the paper, and worked off the lid.

I'd seen the keys to the work trucks often enough to recognize they belonged to a similar model, and my eyes widened as I pulled them out. Unlike the work trucks, it had a proper fob and alarm system, which put it as belonging to a newer vehicle. "Are these the keys to a truck?"

"They're definitely not the keys to a car. After much discussion, I was forced to get you a diesel workhorse because you'd get pissy at the gas trucks, which, according to my sources, would never be able to handle the type of loads you'd be tempted to haul in it once you realize you have your very own manly truck for your personal use."

I could live without mulching Brad's body if I could run him over a few times in a big, manly truck. "You got me a truck?"

"We returned the rental because I was driving you around for the week, and I kept sneaking off while you were working to finalize the paperwork for your new truck. You kept hissing at the rental and complaining it was too dainty, which led me to believe if I wanted to earn your proper favor, I'd secure a proper vehicle for you. You can now mock me that I have to use an FBI vehicle while you romp around in your big, manly truck."

"Where is it? How good do you think it'd be at dragging the body?"

"It's parked somewhere safe, and I'm sure it'd be very good at dragging a body. I'm not entirely unconvinced you can't drag an entire house behind this thing. It's a very big and manly truck."

I decided I could easily listen to him talk about my big, manly truck all day long without complaint. "Tell me more," I demanded.

"It's baby blue because I couldn't bring myself to ask for it to be painted in pink."

"Custom color?"

"Custom color. No flame decals, though. If you want flame decals, you'll have to go to the auto parts store and pick them out yourself. I'm sure you can find some add-ons to get for your big, manly truck using your gift card."

I had the best co-workers, and if Daniel meant to spoil me rotten, he was doing a good job of it. "You told them you were getting me a truck."

"I may have been guilty of such a crime. I asked them what type of truck you would like. I never thought I could trigger the next World War with a question about trucks, but it got pretty intense for a while there. When I finally settled on a model, it got a stamp of approval from your co-workers."

"That's insane."

"It's part of being a lycanthrope. You'll get used to it. And to sweeten the deal in your favor, I may have suggested to the

CDC if they should ear mark part of Brad's settlement fund to cover the full cost of the truck, which was approved as you needed a vehicle and work in the appropriate field. So, not only do you get a really nice truck, technically, Brad had to pay for it."

"So, are you telling me that I'll get to drag Brad's dead body behind a truck you bought me with his money?"

"That sounds about right."

"Is this when I'm supposed to tell you I love you?"

"You can do that whenever you want, however often you want, and wherever you want, but I assumed as much since you'd agreed to marry me. I'm even opting to ignore your primary motivation was securing Brad's dead body."

"I'd consider it a secondary motivation with multiple goals, including getting on with the rest of my life and setting Miranda up with a real man."

"Does that make me your primary motivation?"

I looked him in the eyes and replied, "I haven't felt a burning need to murder you and hide the body. Does that count?"

"You're an evil woman, Emily."

I smiled. "But you like it, and that's what matters, right?"

"You have me figured out. Since you were cruelly forced away from work a day early, what would you like to do today?"

"Let's go on a hunt!"

Daniel laughed. "You just want me to feed you again, don't you?"

"How'd you guess?"

Chapter Eight

WHY DID we bother to make plans? Plans always had a way of failing.

Failure, broken dreams, and unfinished plans littered my life. Some had opened doors, some had closed them, and others diverted me from my original goals and changed me deep inside. I wasn't sure if I believed in fate. Was it fate I'd join forces with my virus to claim the one man we could both agree on? My virus had jumped to conclusions faster than I had, but time had convinced me Daniel was a mistake *I* wanted to make, if I could consider him a mistake. I couldn't. All along, he'd been caught up in the consequences of Brad's actions. We both had our reasons to want revenge. We both wanted to move on. We both wanted to claim some form of happiness.

I found joy in flight and following Daniel, who flew circles around me without trying. Maybe one day I'd grow enough to keep up with him, but I didn't mind chasing after his tail. I appreciated the view, and I could spend hours observing him cut through the air on silent wings.

From the comfort of our apartment, he guided me away from civilization towards the mountains, the ideal place for us to hunt without anyone bothering us. We stopped more often than I thought Daniel liked to give me a chance to catch my breath, and while I recovered, he always brought me a mouse to snack on to keep up my strength. He ate, too, although he always made certain to bring me something first.

I almost blamed the lycanthropy virus for his behavior, but then I realized if he left me to fend for myself, I'd still be on the outskirts of the city hunting for my first snack of the day. When he'd taken me on my first hunt, he'd promised me it would get better. It would take time, but it would get better.

My virus cared less about getting better and more about sticking close to Daniel, and I didn't blame it. The virus viewed the world in a different way than I did. Daniel represented comfort and safety to my virus. I doubted I'd ever get used to the sense of security he'd brought with him when he'd come crashing back into my life.

In time, I'd accept what my virus embraced. It helped Daniel understood I needed time to adapt. Change came in many ways, but I scooted closer to the edge. Tomorrow, I'd fling myself right over a cliff into a new life.

I counted the hours down to my new beginnings and the closure I'd needed for so long. It wouldn't make me a good person, but I'd wear the badge of my sins with pride. Too much hinged on Brad's death.

Miranda deserved better.

So did I.

Our plans faced a critical breakdown when we discovered we weren't the only ones hunting in the mountains. I spotted the wolves first, and they hunted one of their own. I landed on the nearest branch, tense while I observed the hunt below.

Daniel settled behind me and worked his beak into the feathers behind my neck, preening until I relaxed.

When the hunting wolves disappeared through the trees, Daniel bumped me, took flight, and pursued them. I followed, waiting for him to find a new place to land before joining him. The hunting wolves circled their target, and while I suspected their lethal intent, my virus anticipated it, savored the impending violence, and urged me to help out.

We liked the idea of one less wolf in the world.

I reined my virus in and dug my talons into the branch. I would limit my hunt to Brad. I'd be wearing the white dress Daniel had insisted on buying for me along with several others, holding a white crowbar decorated with ribbons. It'd be a gift to my bridesmaid-of-murder as much as a gift to myself.

What other wolves did with each other was no concern to me.

I thought about it, deciding my virus had infected me with a malicious streak a mile wide, since I found the hunt below interesting. Why did they hunt one of their own? Would the wolves play with their prey? I'd always believed wolves to be pack hunters, putting their pack above all else. Did the lone wolf belong to a different pack?

Damn it. Why hadn't I kept a pellet? I could've made so much wonderful mayhem dropping a single pellet into the fray. I fluttered my wings and considered appeasing my virus's desire to play with the wolves. I hopped along the branch, found a small branch, and broke it with a foot, gripping it in my talons.

Daniel hooted at me, and I ignored his disapproval, swooping off my branch with my prize. I aimed for the hunted wolf and dropped the stick on its head.

It howled, leaping in the air and snapping its teeth at me. It came short of catching me, although I hooted my alarm at how high the damned beast could jump.

Stupid wolves.

My virus snapped a lot like the stick had and demanded blood, and I got the feeling it wasn't too picky about who bled as long as it wasn't me. I beat my wings to keep out of the wolf's reach. Either my alarm had gotten under Daniel's skin or he gave up fighting off his virus's instincts, but he dove into the fray and went for the wolf like I went for my first cupcake of the day.

I hadn't realized just how much bigger Daniel was compared to me until he plowed into the wolf and drove him down to the ground in an explosion of fur and feathers. The feathers infuriated my virus, and I dove in to join the fight.

The four wolves joined in, and a mouthful of sharp teeth snagged the back of my head, using enough force to promise a bloody mess probably leading to death. I let loose my shrillest scream and flapped my wings. A pair of paws pressed against my back and pinned me to the ground.

Daniel hopped towards me, spread his wings, and hissed at the wolf who held me.

The other three pounced on the wolf we'd attacked and finished what we'd started, albeit they'd allowed it a chance to fight back before they tore it to pieces, leaving tufts of fur scattered between the trees.

Ew.

"Seriously, you two?" Miranda scolded. "What are you two doing out here? You're supposed to be at your apartment being all lovely dovey. Daniel, you should know better. Taking her out to wolf country? It's like you wanted to teach her how…" She blinked. "Oh. You wanted to teach her how to hunt using prey big enough for her to hit?"

Miranda? I hooted my astonishment, swiveling my head to regard the woman with wide eyes.

Daniel changed directions and hopped to the woman, hooting, chirping, and hissing at her.

"You know I can't understand you when you're an owl. Shift to your hybrid form and explain yourself. I'd say shift to be human, but Emily would get pissy."

I appreciated Miranda acknowledged I would, in fact, get unreasonably upset if she got to see Daniel naked the same time I saw him naked for the first time. We'd kept his modesty fully intact despite him having enjoyed more than a few peeks of me in the nude.

We'd come up with the convenient excuse of him wanting to make sure nothing went wrong with my shifts because I was still far smaller than he liked.

I hadn't seen him in his hybrid form before, and wolves forgotten, I hooted my enthusiasm at her suggestion.

"And you should probably let Emily go before he remembers you're holding her, Luke."

Ah. Luke was one of my favorite of Miranda's potential suitors, a lawyer like her who specialized in family law. He released me, and I hopped to Daniel. When my hooted demands didn't work to make him shift to his hybrid form, I snapped my beak at him.

"I don't need to speak owl to understand she wants you to show off your hybrid form. It's not like you need to save it for her as a wedding present. She knows you have the hybrid form, and it's not like you're going to be getting any hybrid nookie until she develops the form, too. Don't be shy."

Daniel hissed, but he hopped a few steps away from me and shifted, his body growing into a more human, feather-covered shape, his feathers barred to match his more mundane form. His face blended owl and human, his mouth and nose replaced with a beak while he possessed more human eyes. I could understand why he refused to shift into his hybrid form often. Instead of human hands, he had the classic talons of a bird of prey, each sharpened to a lethal point.

Tomorrow, I'd be marrying a living, breathing weapon, and he looked soft enough to use as a pillow.

When had I become a lucky, lucky woman? My virus wanted to secure him as ours immediately, but I ignored it. Tomorrow would do.

Then I'd have a living, breathing pillow that doubled as a weapon all to myself.

Miranda planted her hands on her hips. "Was there any reason you decided to jump into that fight head first?"

Daniel pointed one of his talons at me, and I bristled, hissing at his wordless accusation.

"You can't really deny you participated, Emily. I found it rather amusing your weapon of choice was a stick." Miranda snorted and shook her head. "You have no idea who you helped kill, do you?"

"I do." Daniel clacked his beak, and I blamed his beak for his difficulty with speaking. I could understand him, but I worried if he tried multi-syllable words, I'd struggle to understand him. "Mike."

"His fault for snapping his teeth at your mate. He's been picking up some of Brad's bad habits, and we identified a woman he was targeting. The pack decided to take matters into their own hands. He refused to back off from his plans, and when we warned her, she made it clear she wasn't interested in becoming a lycanthrope. He pushed the point."

"Official?" Daniel swiveled his head to regard Mike's body.

"We caught him in the act. He was planning on spiking her drink to convince her to go home with him. The pack wanted to deal with him. It was approved."

Daniel stared at me. "This is why he wouldn't make his residency California. They treat this harshly. Two or three a year. But he went for you. That would've stood in court."

"We'd told him if he made the Nevada line, he'd get to live but he couldn't return to California." Miranda rolled her shoulders. "Ned wisely decided to leave California, promised to join a good pack, and is being placed by the CDC."

"And Brad?"

"He's going to come here to find out why Mike's dead. These four gentlemen want words with him. I've decided they can have a violent discussion tonight while I watch. You're welcome to watch with me. We made a deal. They will take care of him while I watch. The one who fights the hardest for the right to court me gets his chance."

"Brutal but efficient. I guess you're going to hide the body up here?"

"Seems like a good idea. No one will find them anytime soon."

"This was not our plan, Miranda."

"This plan is better."

"What happened to Emily wearing her dress and her crowbar? I got her a really nice crowbar for this, Miranda."

"She'll like it for work. I'm sure she'll have use for a white crowbar one day. Emily doesn't mind me dealing with the problem myself. Right, Emily?"

I stared at her, stared at him, shook my head, and turned

around, hopping to the wolf I thought was named Luke. I hooted at him.

He translated my call as an invitation to drag his wet tongue over my face.

Wolf breath disgusted me, and I took flight to the nearest branch, hissing over his foul slobber.

"Luke, please don't lick Emily." Daniel clacked his beak and sighed. "You're certain you want to go after Brad tonight, Miranda?"

"I'm certain. He encouraged Mike. He was encouraging Ned, too. Ned hasn't acted yet, but Mike? He'd gone too far. You might want to teach Emily she shouldn't throw sticks at a pack of wolves, though."

"I hadn't thought I needed to suggest she avoid wolves before we went on our flight. She wanted to hunt."

"Next time, perhaps specify wolves aren't on the menu."

"Probably wise. How do you want us to help?"

"You're going to insist, aren't you?"

"Of course."

"You can start with helping us hide the first body."

"If you have a kill authorization, why are you hiding the body?"

"It's more fun that way."

Daniel clacked his teeth. "Does Mike not have any family who will miss him?"

"His home pack disowned him when he kept his alliances with Brad after he went after me and Emily. They're not going to miss him. In fact, when I called his parents to notify him of the kill order, they invited me to a celebration. I also received several offers to help. That's how it goes with wolves, Daniel. Frankly, what we're doing is a mercy. Had we turned him over to his home pack, they would've taken a lot longer to kill him."

I questioned the legal system and its base brutality, but then I considered my virus, which wanted me to join in and take some chunks out of Mike's body and scatter it across the forest. That he'd even considered taking Brad's twisted path infuriated me.

I suspected it was the legal system's way of bowing to the inevitable.

One day, I'd try to figure out where the justice was in murder, but I could—and would—live with the idea we gave a merciful end to those who didn't deserve it.

I would've enjoyed killing Brad, but it would've been quick and brutal rather than long, drawn out, and torturous.

After we killed Brad, hid the body, and made it through my wedding, I'd have to have a long talk with someone about my shady morality. Would Daniel attend sessions with me? I hoped so. He needed some evaluations on his shady morality, too.

In the meantime, I'd go with the flow, count the evening activities as meeting the base requirements for Daniel's challenge to rid the world of Brad, and get to the part I looked forward the most: a new life unburdened by the chains of my past.

I HAD no idea if Daniel could fly while in his hybrid form; he stayed on the ground while helping the wolves deal with Mike's body. In death, he remained a wolf, and I developed a healthy respect for Daniel's talons, which did an admirable and efficient job of tearing through flesh and bone alike.

I preened my feathers while watching the festivities below. The wolves dug so many holes they left the forest a tilled mess, and bits of body went into each one. Then, to make it even more difficult on investigators, they churned up the soil as far as I could see in any direction. Maybe one day someone would find Mike's body, but if they did, I doubted anyone would think to test for human DNA in shattered wolf bones.

Once finished, Daniel shifted back to an owl, joined me on my branch, and worked his beak into my feathers, grooming me to his satisfaction. It intrigued me Mike's blood hadn't survived through shifting; it didn't for me, either, which had helped make my life much easier when in hiding. That dirt remained meant magic of some form.

Maybe one day I'd ask Daniel if I'd inherited some odd magical ability from him or if all lycanthropes purged blood from their coats or feathers when transforming.

"All right. Brad's on the move and headed this way," Miranda announced, pointing through the trees. "He's coming from that direction. Daniel, you're our scout. Locate him, return, and guide the pack to his position. Emily, you stick with me. I know you'd rather like to help, but you'll go for his face, and we need the pack in position before you take any dives for him."

I appreciated that Miranda understood I'd be getting in my hits despite leaving the majority of the work to the wolves so they could earn her favor. I wouldn't even do more than get my talons a little bloody.

She needed the closure and new hopes for the future far more than I did.

Daniel hooted and took to the air, winging away in the direction she pointed.

"If we're lucky, he'll be a wolf, which is probable. It's a lot easier to hide a wolf's body. Unless there's reason to believe it's a lycanthrope, no one thinks to do anything more than a general species check when examining the bones, and lycanthrope wolves register as a mundane wolf when shifted. It's only if they run additional scans they'll pick up the lycanthropy virus, and most aren't interested in testing animal bodies. It works in our benefit. If we'd waited for tomorrow, we'd have to either relinquish the body for proper burial or try to hide a human body. That's much more difficult."

I glided off my branch and landed beside Miranda, fluffing my feathers and settling in to wait.

Miranda's wolves drew close, and except for a few licks, they ignored me and focused on her.

I almost pitied Brad. Four wolves vying for Miranda's attention would leave nothing but tufts of fur and scraps by the time they finished fighting over the body to impress her. No matter which one won, I'd sleep better knowing she'd be in good hands—or paws—until she and her virus recovered from Brad's death.

I hoped her virus proved somewhat sensible and picked one of the four contenders sooner than later.

It didn't take long for Daniel to return, and he circled until the wolves followed him, moving through the underbrush in eerie silence.

"Brad must be close for Daniel to have found him so quickly." Miranda snorted. "Typical. He stalks me, always."

He wouldn't for much longer. I took to the air and circled around Miranda, following her slower march through the forest. She lifted her chin, but I couldn't tell if she wanted to convince the world her pride remained intact or if she steeled herself for the price she'd pay for her mate's death.

I heard the growls before I caught sight of Daniel perched

on a high branch. His attention remained fixed on the ground below. Joining him, I followed his gaze.

I recognized Brad from the scars on his muzzle, his fur streaked white from where I'd torn into him. Miranda's hopeful courters circled him, and while Brad growled and snapped his teeth, the others fell quiet. In their silence I heard their willingness to kill.

I wanted to get in my blows, but I clutched the branch and remained with Daniel.

I'd done my part, and moving on meant letting go.

It didn't take Miranda's wolves long to tear Brad apart, and long after his death, they fought over his body while she watched in silence.

It took us until dusk to collect Brad's remains and give him a burial. As expected, Brad's death hit Miranda hard but not in the way any of us expected.

Grief, I supposed, took many forms. Miranda laughed until she cried, and when she couldn't cry any more, she fell prey to her rage, cursing Brad for everything he'd done to her. She started from the night he'd ruined her life, leaving no stone unturned about how he'd treated her.

To my guilt and shame, my first reaction was to be grateful it hadn't been me. I'd lost my humanity to him, too, but I'd escaped his trap. Daniel's love, unbeknownst to me then, had triumphed over Brad's virus, clinging to me and giving me wings when I needed them the most.

Daniel kept his word to help remove Brad from my life, shifting to his hybrid form and handling most of the disposal. I counted his contribution, which often involved helping the wolves dig countless holes and tear up the forest floor to make Brad's final resting place a secret.

Between the five of them, they tore up so much ground it'd take searchers months to find even one of the holes containing Brad's bones.

Covered in dirt with his head bowed with weariness, Daniel hopped to Miranda. "Do you need more time?"

His question drew the woman up short, and she blinked as though realizing she hadn't been alone during her tirade. She turned in a slow circle, taking in the torn ground and the removal of any sign of Brad's brutal but quick demise. "No. I've given him too much time as it is."

Daniel rose to his full height, towering over Miranda, and he stroked his beak over her hair, careful not to scour her with the curved tip. I recognized his preening as an owl's way of offering comfort, platonic yet intimate. My virus didn't mind, nor did I.

Enough damage had been done for one night.

"Your males will be at the wedding tomorrow, dressed properly as a candidate worthy of you. Tonight, you come home with Emily, and you two will become princesses for a night. To make sure they do this, I will accompany them for the night. We will discuss their prowess in detail, and you will decide which you want after the wedding. You and Emily can bury your pasts, enjoy the bottle of wine I've stashed in the fridge for your enjoyment, and do whatever it is women do when sharing space temporarily. I just ask you don't break the apartment."

"We're not going to break the apartment, Dan."

"Good. Tonight is your night to grieve. Tomorrow, things will be better, and when the curious ask, you can just shrug and suggest Brad had finally bitten off more than he could chew. Do make sure you specify you don't care what had happened to him. Try to make sure my bride gets into her dress and shows up without incident. I'm trusting her with you."

"And I'm trusting you to bring all four of my wolves tomorrow."

"One to be your mate, the rest to be your pack?"

Miranda rolled her eyes. "I'll have enough trouble keeping up with one as my mate. Three extras would drive us all insane. We've come to an understanding."

"Good. I hope you can convince Emily to forgive me for robbing her of the ability to run over Brad's body in her new truck."

"Ah, gave her the keys already?"

"I figured you could drive her to the wedding site in her new truck. I'll bring it around after we get in."

"Why don't we all just head over to the site tonight? We'll call it a pack sleep over, and don't you give me any shit about being owls. Our pack is more than happy to welcome a pair of owls into the fold."

Daniel faced me, staring at me in silent questioning.

Did he think I'd say no? I had no love for some wolves, but I had plenty of affection for Miranda. I hooted and bobbed my head.

"She seems game, so sure. I'll go get the truck and meet you at the end of the road. We may as well give her the next present tonight."

"Sounds good."

I understood why so many plans had changed the instant

Daniel turned my bright baby blue Chevy Silverado onto the street leading to the little dead-end road I'd once called home. Once upon a time, the lot had been my dream, a place with enough woods and hills nearby to satisfy my virus.

The last time I'd seen it, there'd been nothing but charred waste left. I hadn't had much of a house, but it'd been mine, and I'd lost it.

Someone had built the American dream on the lot with a white picket fence around a backyard, opting for a rock garden over grass and brush ripe for burning. To keep the property from being completely barren, someone had brought in and planted fruit trees, and several of them were large enough for us to perch in if we wanted.

"You fixed it?" I whispered, and the tears I refused to shed choked off my voice.

"The land and house were yours, and you had the property taxes on auto-withdraw. It's been waiting for you to come home, and it seemed like leaving it to rot would be a worse crime. After the wildfire, the neighbors sold the land; the lots were still for sale, so I got a mortgage for the land." Daniel parked the truck in the driveway and pointed to where my property had once ended. "I got three lots along that way for ten acres, there's an extra ten acres in the back, and don't ask me how many acres I got on the other side of the property. Miranda helped me negotiate for the land so I could afford it."

Daniel had done *what*? Stunned, I unbuckled my seatbelt and slid out of my truck, seeing the land with new eyes. With ten acres on one side, more than he was comfortable announcing on the other, and the backyard I'd always wanted but hadn't been able to afford, everything I could see in the darkness belonged to me. No, to us. "How much was it?"

"Too much," he admitted.

"Does my settlement cover it?"

Miranda laughed. "She doesn't like debt, Daniel. Just view your gift as making the arrangements so she can buy it. That can be her gift to you."

"And we're having the wedding *here*?"

"It would've been a little tacky, even for us, to kill that bastard in our backyard. But yes, the wedding will be here. Your boss, who will be at the wedding tomorrow, along with the rest of your co-workers, thought it might be too much of a shock if we surprised you too much at one time. He hadn't realized your house had burned in the wildfire because you kept working like always and hadn't seemed bothered by anything. The crew came over to make sure everything was ready, make certain the back was set up for tomorrow, and checked over everything inside. My job was to take you to work, help keep you distracted with presents, and keep you busy until after dark. That's when Miranda cooked up the idea to lure Mike and Brad into the hills."

"You took us there on purpose."

Daniel killed the engine and hopped out of my truck. "I told you we had a new plan for his death. I just neglected to mention we'd moved the timetable up and went with simple, brutal, and remote. Now that we're cleared out, a few friends are going to go to the spot and encourage the forest to grow a bit to make the whole area look undisturbed. If anyone wants to find them, they'll have to dig up that entire mountain."

Miranda and her wolves hopped out of the bed of my truck and headed for the front door, and Miranda took out a set of keys and jingled them. "You two lover birds take your time. I'll give Jacob a call and ask him to come around with the clothes and let him know you two are here."

They disappeared inside, leaving me alone with Daniel.

"Have I met your challenge to your satisfaction, Emily?"

"You have. Miranda looks happy."

"She'll have a few bad weeks because of her virus, but yes. She's going to be happy."

"Know which wolf is going to win her?"

"Of course. Everyone's known for a while which one would. Tonight really wasn't about them confirming who'd be her mate but making it clear they'd stand together to bring her into their pack."

"Which one won?"

"Luke, of course. That's why I didn't rip his face off for touching you. He's going to be happily mated soon enough I could tolerate him near you. That was part of our plan, too."

"You're a devious man."

"I'll be anything you need me to be."

I could only think of one thing to tell him, and I smiled. "Be yourself. That's what I really need."

"Gladly." Daniel offered his arm. "Shall we?"

The rest of my life looked like it was off to a good start, and I linked my arm with his so he could show me the world he'd built for me from the charred ruins of my past.

About the Author

Want to hear more from the author? Sign up for the Sneaky Kitty Critic's newsletter!

RJ BLAIN suffers from a Moleskine journal obsession, a pen fixation, and a terrible tendency to pun without warning.

When she isn't playing pretend, she likes to think she's a cartographer and a sumi-e painter.

In her spare time, she daydreams about being a spy. Should that fail, her contingency plan involves tying her best of enemies to spinning wheels and quoting James Bond villains until she is satisfied.

RJ also writes as Susan Copperfield and Trillian Anderson.

If you enjoy using bookbub, you can follow RJ and her alter ego Susan there.

http://thesneakykittycritic.com

Magical Romantic Comedies (with a body count)

Playing with Fire

Hoofin' It

Hearth, Home, and Havoc

Whatever for Hire

Serial Killer Princess

Owl Be Yours

Fowl Play (Sept 2018)

No Kitten Around (Oct 2018)

Blending In (Nov 2018)

Cheetahs Never Win (Dec 2018)

Saddle Up (2019)

Grave Humor (May 2019)

Dragon Her Heels (Late 2019)

CPSIA information can be obtained
at www.ICGtesting.com
Printed in the USA
FSHW020725300919
62512FS

9 781949 740080